TRIF3CTA

THREE STORIES OF
SPECULATIVE CONTACT

STONEY COMPTON

PULLO PUP PUBLISHING LLC

Willamette Valley, Oregon

Also by Stoney Compton

RUSSIAN AMERIKA
ALASKA REPUBLIK
TREADWELL: A NOVEL OF ALASKA TERRITORY
THANE, THE ASSASSINATION OF WARREN G.
HARDING
WHALESONG
LEVEL SIX
RETURN TO KIANA
INCIDENT IN ALASKA PREFECTURE
TWILIGHT OF EMPIRE

all are available on Amazon.com

for the latest on Stoney's writing,
or to make comments on this book, go to:

http://www.stoneycompton.com

Tabu was originally published as *When The Ship Came* in *Tomorrow, Speculative Fiction*, Vol 12 (1994).

Trappers was originally published in *Jim Baen's Universe*, (2010).

For more information about the author go to:
http://www.stoneycompton.com
Give us a "Like" at:
http://www.facebook.com/pullo.pup.publishing

ISBN-978-0-9906395-6-5

Cover by Stoney Compton

Dedicated
with love and great respect
to my oldest, most constant amigo,
ally, and partner in adventure,

Delmar Francis Buhrman

Trappers

Stoney Compton

The idea for *Trappers* was the result of a sketch I made while listening to a geology lecture in college. The image (wish I still had it!) was of a tripodal creature with a nasty looking weapon waiting on a snow-covered rise for the mountain man tracking it to show himself. The image and possible sequence of events stayed with me for over thirty years before I finally sat down and wrote the story. This story previously appeared in *Jim Baen's Universe*, edited by my friend Eric Flint.

Trappers

1

Tightly gripping his .58 Hawken, Caleb Pasco eased into the icy creek. His keen gaze moved from bank to bank as his moccasin-clad feet felt their way across the pebbly bottom. Ahead of him the stake anchoring his trap protruded from the rippling water.

Took the bait, he thought, *now let's see what I got.*

Constantly scanning both banks, he ran his left hand down the stake and found the chain, hefted it and made a low whistle.

"By the almighty, this here's a big 'un." He continued watching the woods on either side of the creek. Blackfoot seldom announced their presence with aught but an arrow.

With practiced motions he slid the steel ring up the stake and towed the beaver carcass to the bank where his two horses waited. Caleb looked away from the surrounding trees long enough to free the mangled leg of the drowned rodent. He knew it didn't pay to open traps without minding your work.

He let his eyes rest on the animal for a long moment before glancing around.

If this don't beat all. Just when I thought all the streams in these mountains was done played out, I find this place.

It just didn't calculate. This creek wasn't that far off the well traveled trails. Just two years ago his old friend, Jim Bridger, had built himself a trading post on Black's Fork of the Green River not three days steady travel from here. The beaver had played out long before that.

He let himself reflect on the heady days of the '20s and early '30s when he and the beaver were in their prime. Behind him, his horse snorted, bringing Caleb's gaze sweeping over the tree line. He dropped the trap and cocked the Hawken.

Spring had nearly trumped winter, new leaves hovered at bud stage, but dirty snow stubbornly lingered in shaded clefts. Nothing moved. He eased back to where his horses stood tied to a cottonwood. Clark, his mount, possessed more brains than Lewis, his packhorse.

Clark's ears twitched, and his eyes rolled from side to side. *Spooked*, Caleb decided, *but by man or beast?*

Ta'ffil ceased forward movement, thrillingly appreciative of the alert perception of one of the quadruped creatures she previously perceived as non-sapient. Slowly Ta'ffil extended a limb up into the massive celluloid stalk beside her, wrapped it about a horizontal division and pulled herself up into the juncture. The alpha creature clutched a chemical projectile weapon and peer about with its unenhanced primitive receptors.

Barely sapient, she decided.

It looked at her, and she swiftly modified her skin to match the mottled green protuberances around her. The slave creature wiggled its antennae in Ta'ffil's direction. She considered retreat to her craft. Her mission concerned fuel, not the collection of yet another intelligent alien, but there was the wager.

The alpha creature touched the slave creature. "What's the matter, Clark?" Its clacking made no sense to her, not even registering in the upper frequencies where her species communicated.

The alpha creature continued twisting its sensory appendage back and forth, futilely seeking reason for the beta creature's discomfort. Ta'ffil's neural net oscillated between superiority and disdain. Her symbiote, Na'znn, was about to lose the mock wager between them.

The now-sure acquisition of this creature would put her two captures ahead of him. A swift tendril of glee pulsed through her. A ripple in the atmosphere abruptly claimed her attention.

The alpha creature stood beneath the celluloid stalk refuge and seemed to be regarding her.

"What the blue blazes is that, Clark?"

Despite the creature's ability to perceive only a limited spectrum, Ta'ffil realized it really saw her. She sent limbs upward while altering her chroma to match the rough textured cellulose.

Fear-tinged humiliation replaced superiority as she tried to meld with the plant, pushing her mass as close to integration with the stalk as possible. Her chroma now matched the rough exterior. Perhaps the creature would lose sight of her.

"Jehoshaphat, Clark, that critter just turned into a piece of tree!"

Ta'ffil sensed awe in the polyglot nuances. Her superiority and elation flared anew as the creature suddenly hurried around the area, picking up unattached pieces of celluloid lying on the planet surface. Perhaps it intended to treat her as a deity, bend to her superior intelligence and abilities?

Still moving quickly, the creature carefully piled the loose celluloid around the base of her hiding-stalk. Ta'ffil's high emotion abruptly plummeted as the creature created sparks from objects grasped in its appendages. A smoke cilia wafted past her as small tongues of flame crept into the piled celluloid.

Ta'ffil realized her extreme peril and opened her sensory capability to maximum. No other stalks stood close enough to allow safe transfer. If she descended to the planet surface the creature would surely do her harm, and her nulgrav lay in her scout ship.

The flames rapidly oxidized the loose pieces. Heat rose and Ta'ffil experienced a ripple of panic that she instantly quashed. Quickly she ranged through her short span of options.

Retreat without the nulgrav would be useless. The Race could approach an enemy undetected without equipage. However, being conquerors, their retreats wanted mechanical aid.

She must descend or be consumed by the growing fire.

With hope of reflecting as much thermal radiation as possible, she altered her chroma to nil. Her mantle became chitinous, complete with defense points, and she felt the sharp hooks form in her locomotive limbs. The heat intensified and, with no other option left, she launched herself at the creature.

3

Caleb watched the thing turn white, thought maybe he'd killed it already. But it kept changing. He felt his hackles lift when the critter suddenly turned hard with sharp points rising out of its back.

Anything that hides in a tree at the edge of a man's camp has to be up to no good. Not to mention this thing was so skin crawling different from anything he had ever seen before, and he'd seen plenty. He reached over and grabbed his Hawken, holding it ready, just in case—

The critter suddenly snapped out of the tree at him like a flat tailless painter, shrilling like the banshees his momma told him about decades ago. Caleb instantly shouldered the Hawken and shot the critter dead center.

The heavy caliber ball went right through it, causing it to fall short — onto a bucking, screaming, firmly tied Lewis. The critter flopped on the horse like a slimy wet blanket, thrusting claws into the animal's body.

Lewis shrieked and jumped so hard all four hooves cleared the ground. The horse twisted in the air, desperately trying to throw the critter, biting at it. Then Lewis came down on his neck, snapping it with a loud crack.

"You sonuvabitch!" Caleb bellowed at the critter, racing over to Clark to get his horse pistol. Clark's eyes rolled whitely and froth ringed his nostrils as he lunged against the rope holding him to the fallen cottonwood. The tree had already gouged six feet of dirt.

"Clark, Clark," Caleb called, trying to sooth the horse but unable to disguise the fear and excitement in himself. He grabbed the reins and jerked hard, hating himself for hurting the animal.

Clark stopped jerking for a moment, his sides heaving and running with sweat. Caleb jerked open the pannier and grabbed the thick-handled pistol.

Cocking it while turning, he raced back to the mound of flesh he once called Lewis. The critter slowly slipped off the dead horse, oozing something black, no, dark green, Caleb decided.

As Caleb neared the critter, it stopped and bunched up on itself, raising its closest side slightly into the air. He shook powder into the pistol pan, took careful aim at the middle part, and fired.

A bright eye of fire suddenly appeared in its mass. The ball knocked the critter backward and part of it fell on the fire. It shrilled again, but not as loud as the first time, and slowly began pulling its parts out of the flames.

All Caleb had left was his skinning knife and the trap he'd pulled off the beaver. Instantly he grabbed the chain and swung the trap over and down on the critter as hard as he could. It shuddered like a gut-shot buffalo, trying to edge away.

Caleb, grinning like a madman, swung the trap again.

Ta'ffil neared insanity from the waves of agony. The heavy projectiles had torn through her assimilation organ and the plexus controlling locomotion. She knew this creature had killed her.

Her scout craft lay hidden only a few multiples away on the fuel deposit she was to collect. Although it might as well be in orbit with the alpha ship for all it could offer her now. The Prime Maxim from her training burned through her agonized mind.

She touched her command pad, rippling code into it as quickly as possible. The heavy thing smashed into her again and she felt her consciousness ebbing. She rippled the last sequence and, with a feeling of victorious loss, died.

Caleb pulled the trap back and started to swing again. Three hundred feet up-slope, a tremendous explosion tore a hole in the mountain. Sixty-foot trees blew into flinders, and the shock wave knocked both man and horse off their feet. The burning tree slammed to the ground, barely missing Caleb, but obliterating the critter.

Caleb and Clark scrambled to their feet. The horse no longer tried to flee, but remained agitated. Caleb tried to see what the critter looked like, but pitch popped and snapped out of the burning fir tree, completely engulfing the creature.

Caleb edged back from the heat.

"What the hell? Nobody will believe this one. They'll think I'm a bigger liar than Coulter when he first told 'em about the Yellowstone country."

He turned and walked to Clark, ran his hands over the shuddering horse. "It's all right, Clark. It's all over now."

Na'znn abruptly regained full cognizance as the gel nest's pulse shifted to an irritating stutter. He silenced the alarm and caused the nest to expel him. Deftly spurting through the ship he caught a junction rod and changed direction without losing momentum.

Coming to rest at the pilot console, he scanned the readouts. The automatic communication link to Ta'ffil's craft had ceased. The only way the link could be mute was to destroy the scout craft itself.

Desolation and loss swept through him. Her essence now ranged beyond comprehension somewhere in the Transfer Plane. Why? How?

On their outward journey through this sector they had located a massive amount of fuel on this planet and placed a stasis field over the source. A thorough exploration revealed none of the primitive sapient creatures, and what sentient life existed inside the field would not suffer for the exclusion of outside creatures.

Only the arrival of Ta'ffil's scout craft could negate the field, so nothing could have been lying in wait for her.

This sudden new situation lacked symmetry and Na'znn felt confused anger.

Self-preservation told him to leave this planet and continue toward home. Emotion cried for revenge against whatever had taken the essence of his symbiote. He ignored both. He must accede to the needs of the ship with its cargo of information and specimens.

Without the fuel supply on the planet's surface, the ship could not reach home. They had carefully extended their outward journey only after locating adequate fuel deposits on planets and asteroids they encountered along the way. Na'znn engaged the long-range sensors.

Ta'ffil's craft had self-destructed directly over the fuel deposit, vaporizing a third of the soft, pure metal.

He quickly calculated the remainder and discovered he needed almost all of it to return home safely. Now he must consider why Ta'ffil perished. Although he reveled in her seasonal sexual embrace, there had been much about the younger female that displeased him.

Impetuous to a fault, aggressive, and smug, she seldom considered the possible negative consequences of her actions. Her mental acuity ranked second to none, which accounted for her presence on this mission. While cogitating, he methodically set the ship for unattended duty, prepared the remaining scout craft for departure, and considered beginning the dirge for a fallen comrade.

Automatically, he directed a visual orb over the read-outs monitoring the specimen hold. All hovered close to death, locked in deep stasis.

After his return he would complete the rites for a lost symbiote. Now he didn't have the luxury of time. Without further ado he slipped through the auxiliary bay hatch and sealed it behind him.

The empty berth, which Ta'ffil's ship would never again fill, mocked him, giving him pause and heightening his grief. Moments later his scout craft emerged from the alpha ship and angled toward the bright blue-green planet below.

Caleb's mind seethed with questions as he finished quartering Lewis. At least the animal wouldn't go to waste. Caleb had acquired a taste for horseflesh during his first winter with the Shoshone, twenty, twenty-five years ago.

"You ain't quite as sweet as buff, but you'll do," he muttered to the meat while slicing flesh and expertly separating bones at the joints. All the while, his mind pondered the last three days.

The sudden discovery of a new valley had put him into a frazzle to begin with. He'd been through these parts a couple dozen times in the past forty years and he'd never seen this stream. A valley like this should have been one of the first to get picked clean.

Old Ned Bedlam had been one of those philosopher types before getting rubbed out by the Blackfoot. Claiming formal schooling from back east, he'd called the other trappers "fine examples of noble men, free-living and pure." He also talked about how these mountains had formed and the creeks, streams, and rivers had cut valleys and all.

Of course Caleb and the other mountain men had laughed hugely at his stories and pronouncements in genuine appreciation. But Caleb listened hard just the same, and he never forgot any of the things Old Ned told him. As far as Caleb knew, these mountains and streams had been here since Lucifer was a pup, unchanging and unchangeable.

However since then he'd noticed how things slowly did change; new channels cut in streams, oxbows cut off and left to dry up. Even the mountains changed slowly.

But new valleys didn't just happen. Three-year-old beaver didn't show up plump and sassy in an area where skittish one-year-olds were hard to find, let alone trap.

Caleb finished his butchering, wishing he had time to smoke the meat. He salted down the hide, folded it and tied it with his pile of beaver pelts. Clark would have to carry the hides and traps.

Caleb would walk out of the mountains this summer. That meant an early start. Although once he finished with this creek, there probably wouldn't be anything else worth lollygagging about anyway.

He was leaving the mountains for good. Forty years of "pure, free living" had taken their toll, eroding his optimism and hubris down to mere shadows of their former selves. He wanted at least a decade of soft, civilized life before he died.

Last summer he'd tied the remains of Talking Woman, his Nez Perce wife, into a scaffold in a tree far up in the Grand Tetons. At first he didn't want the bother of another wife, but after a winter sleeping alone, he'd softened his mind. A nice, soft, plump little dumpling of a lady would be just the ticket to keep his bony ass warm through his remaining winters.

He eyed the pile of ashes left from the burnt tree, and lifted his gaze to where the explosion had bit a chunk out of the mountain. After a long thought he picked up his Hawken and moved cautiously up the slope.

The hole yawned widely, scooped out of solid rock on a small plateau. An unfamiliar stink hung in the air. In an odd way, Caleb decided, it smelled somewhat of heated metal, like a blacksmithy.

Something glinted at him from the hole. He surveyed every direction, taking his time, looking for movement, before deciding he could chance a quick trip to the bottom.

He tested every step with his toes, knowing a broken leg could mean a hard death. He reached the bottom and peered at the bright spot in the wall, a gouge in the wide band undulating across the face of the torn rock. After carving out a blob with his knife, Caleb examined it carefully.

Wonder flooded through him as he realized he had discovered a large vein of pure gold.

Na'znn allowed the planet's rotation to cloak the fuel deposit in darkness before landing nearby. He prepared the scout craft; activating the security and intruder systems, as well as the stasis shield, watching to ensure it redirected all local spectra. To the uninitiated, the small ship became invisible.

Unlike the younger and more adventurous Ta'ffil, Na'znn wore his nulgrav unit. No creeping about for him. She had mocked him in the past for using technology that gave him an advantage over local beings. Her adolescent games probably contributed to her death.

He refused to dwell on her void; the journey home would not be quick. Na'znn nullified local gravity and expertly caught the prevailing breeze to carry him to the fuel deposit. In less time than required for a mate-meld, he neared the fuel.

The scent of fresh fuel in the nitrogen-rich atmosphere pushed his ancient warrior-brain into the forefront of his reason. Following orders, Ta'ffil had landed directly over the deposit. The self-destruction of her craft had cost him a great deal.

Na'znn pulsed the nulgrav to stasis and settled near the gaping hole reeking of fuel and glowing strangely. The remaining task of placing the molecular transfer would take moments. Suddenly, a creature from the depths of his worst night-knots, illuminated from below, rose from the hole in front of him.

Caleb's body ran with sweat by the time he tossed the first two beaver skin bags of gold out of the hole. They made satisfying thuds. He grinned into the darkness, knew he was a fool to be mining at night. However the Blackfoot didn't roam after dark.

He dropped back into the hole to stare at the seam of gold in the wavering light of his small fire. Just the sight of it made his heart speed. After years in the mountains living hand-to-mouth he now found himself rich.

Visions of a mansion in St. Louis wafted through his mind. Forgetting the plump little lady, he saw himself surrounded by beautiful, young, alabaster-skinned women in fancy dresses, all vying for his attention. They would smell of perfume instead of wood smoke, buckskin, and bad teeth.

The notion of it made him light headed, nearly putting him in a faint.

"By the almighty," he muttered, "I can have anything I want. Nothing can stand in the way of wealth like this. I'll never have to worry about having enough meat."

He attacked the seam again, gouging out the soft, flawless metal with his heavy knife. The next two bags filled quickly. He tied them off with sinew and arched his back to relieve the ache.

"This is harder than trapping," he said with a groan. He grinned, realizing that each bag held at least the equivalent of three year's wages. This had happened at the right time, too, on his way out of the mountains.

He carried the two bags up and tossed them on the ground next— the first two bags weren't there. Instinctively, he grabbed his Hawken, cocking the heavy hammer as he brought it level with his waist, aiming into the night. Nothing moved.

No human could have snuck up and taken the bags, not that quickly. Caleb's senses heightened as his eyes adjusted to the dark. Nothing broke the skyline. Every shadow remained stationary in the warm night.

Sweat slid down his forehead, dripped off his nose. His eyes inched over memorized ground. Tension built in his chest.

The only thing that could have taken the gold was one of those critters. Nothing else could move silently enough to be undetectable to his trained ears.

"Why would something like that want gold?" Caleb asked aloud.

A tremor of hysterical mirth rose in him and he held it back, not allowing it freedom. Not since his expedition days in Blackfoot country had he been this frightened.

He'd been an eighteen-year-old private with the party of Meriwether Lewis when the Field brothers had knifed a Blackfoot to death in an argument gone bad, forever cursing the white race with an implacable foe. Remembering that frantic, mad dash the party made down through Blackfoot territory, until finally making contact with the force Clark led, had kept him looking over his shoulder to this day for the roached hair and hard, glittering eyes. Now with spring fully underway, the young bucks would be ready for stealing horses and women, and happily killing any *washicu* they happened across.

This fear was different. He understood the Blackfoot. He didn't understand this.

He eased off one foot and onto the other. The Hawken seemed to want to slip out of his sweaty hands and he strengthened his grip. He had been lucky to kill the last one.

He hoped his luck would hold.

Na'znn flowed into the hole as the creature left, flattening himself against the cold, bare mineral wall, quickly adopting its texture and chroma. He retained the small clutches of fuel. Exactly what did the creature mean by its act?

Had this creature caused Ta'ffil's death and now offered the fuel as an act of atonement? Or had the creature witnessed the death of Na'znn's companion and thought them superior beings? If the act was an offering, why did the creature advance and brandish a weapon?

While parsing coherency from the confusion offered, Na'znn became aware of the creature's oral communications.

"It don't float, Clark. What would a walking porcupine rug want with gold?"

Na'znn determined that the creature spoke to the quadruped. It didn't seem sapient, but definitely sentient. While the first creature communicated, the second creature stared fixedly at the hole. Na'znn retracted the pseudopod, altering the cells from sensory to protection.

Na'znn flowed over to the thick streak of fuel and anchored the molecular transfer node. With a slight tick, the apparatus began converting the mineral into plasma. Almost instantly the transfer beam hummed in the air between hole and scout craft, glowing redly as fuel plasma began flowing across the space.

"What the hell!" The creature suddenly loomed over the hole, weapon pointing at the molecular transfer. "It's eating up my gold?"

Before Na'znn could react, the creature lifted its weapon and a sensory-withering blast smashed the molecular transfer node into atoms. He adapted his coloration to fit the cold wall, feeling exposed and vulnerable.

The beam winked out of existence and fuel thudded to the planet surface in a long glistening line pointing toward the hidden scout craft.

The creature hurried to the soft metal and grabbed a fragment, then quickly dropped it, waving one appendage in the air.

"Shee-it!" It bellowed. "This gold's hotter'n banked coals!"

Na'znn realized the creature also wanted the fuel; there had been no offering, no contrition for killing his mate.

After extending a visual orb over the lip of the hole to ascertain the creature's location, Na'znn flowed out into the surrounding plants undetected. From his concealment, he watched the creature make piles of loose celluloid equidistant around the hole and then transfer them into bright, hot oxidization.

Na'znn knew a defensive perimeter when he saw one. He realized war had been declared. Rippling commands into his nulgrav, he lifted silently into the night.

Caleb added fuel to the fires and peered about in the dark. The gold vein glinted invitingly from the hole. Nothing stirred in the surrounding area.

He slipped into the hole and quickly began gouging gold from the vein, letting it fall into the bottom of the pit. He would collect it later. Rather than worrying about every ounce freed from the wall, he would dig as much as possible and collect what he could.

He realized there must be another creature out there, and this one was smarter than the first. Faced with actual wealth and the opportunity to spend his last years being totally profligate, one the best words Ned Bedlam ever taught him, he wasn't going to run from this. The new critter would have to best him.

Every few minutes he would drop his knife, grab his Hawken and survey the area around the hole. Nothing. He went back to the vein.

Dawn washed over the eastern horizon by the time Caleb finished filling his sacks with gold. Exhaustion weighted every fiber of his being, and his hands shook as he set the bags on the rim of the hole. Finally, he grabbed his Hawken and clambered out to sit and survey the surrounding area.

He was so tired he could barely keep his eyes open. But he knew if he let his guard down now, he might lose everything he had mined during the night. He didn't know why the critter wanted the gold, but why didn't matter; the fact was enough.

Caleb added fuel to all the fires and hurried over to where Clark waited. The horse followed the lead readily, which told Caleb that no critter lurked in the area. Within a quarter of an hour he had his panniers packed with the small fortune.

His confidence climbed to new heights. Certain wealth gave a man a stiffer spine. For the first time the thought of trapping the critter crossed his mind.

Na'znn scouted the hole at three multiples, safely concealed behind the celluloid stalks ringing the site. The creature had departed. Immediately he flowed into the hole and measured the fuel lode.

The remainder proved inadequate for the ship's needs. The creature had taken an amazing amount of the metal during the dark phase. Na'znn cautiously circled the primitive dwelling where the creature lay.

When he neared six multiples of the shelter, the quadruped became highly agitated, jerking at its lashing and emitting high-pitched sounds. Na'znn reversed his course immediately and settled among the celluloid stalks. The creature stumbled out of its shelter, chemical-projectile-weapon at the ready.

"What's wrong Clark, the critter back?" He peered around the small clearing. He rubbed at his visual sensors, the weapon in his other hand wavered.

"Damn, but I need me some sleep." The weapon sagged. "Keep watch, Clark, I can't do more right now."

Na'znn watched the creature vanish into his small shelter. He fastened his attention on the quadruped. If he could eliminate the ancillary creature, he could easily surprise and eliminate or capture the alpha creature.

A cilia of new self-realization flashed though him. He realized a part of him wanted to capture the creature that killed his symbiote. The other specimen now held in stasis on the ship were intelligent or dangerous in their own right, but they hadn't come close to killing a member of his race. Taking the creature back to his home planet would achieve symmetry.

The quadruped ate at the small ground-cover cellulose but continually lifted its head to stare in Na'znn's direction. There would be no surprising this creature unless he attacked from above.

He couldn't use the weapons on the scout ship for fear of destroying the shelter and the collected fuel along with the two creatures. He would have sink to more primitive means to realize his objective. The heavy gravity of this planet would become an ally.

Na'znn found a piece of worthless mineral roughly the size of the alpha creature's head and extruded appendages around it. Once he had a firm grip, he flowed commands into his nulgrav. The device lifted him slowly, humming at the extra load.

He knew he must gain many multiples to rise above the quadruped's awareness. The personal nulgrav was not designed to lift as much as a large material-handler. It now generated enough heat to make Na'znn uncomfortable physically as well as mentally.

He couldn't gain the elevation he wished. Perhaps he was high enough? At the maximum speed he could achieve he came at the creature from behind, hoping its hearing was not as keen as its smell and vision.

Mere seconds before his calculated release of the crude missile, the quadruped jerked at its lashing and jumped to the side, eyes rolling whitely and shrilling loudly. The alpha creature burst from its shelter, quickly determining the direction of the quadruped's alarm. The creature aimed its weapon at Na'znn, shouted, "Went for the bait, didn't ya?" and fired at the same moment Na'znn launched the rock into its trajectory.

The creature's projectile hit the waste material as Na'znn's nulgrav, free of the massive load, immediately pulled him upward in a rapid climb. He steered it back toward the largest stand of celluloid and came to rest high in the thin appendages of the tallest specimen he could find.

A combination of fear and respect coalesced in his mind as he realized this creature was a worthy opponent — exactly what he did not need at this stage of his homeward journey. Their search had borne success unimaginable. They had found two worlds where they thought their race could prosper unthreatened.

Na'znn found it bitter that this world was half of their discovery. He faced vast distances before he could rest, and no early-chemical-era creature was going to stop him.

Caleb sat in shock, staring at his mangled left leg. The rock had shattered the knee and most of the leg beneath it. He knew if the leg didn't come off immediately, he would die, that he might anyway.

"Didn't realize I was using my leg as bait…"

The critter hadn't pressed its advantage, flying away as quick as any bat or swift. How long would it be before the thing took advantage of his debilitation?

Struggling to remain conscious he wrapped a leather thong around his thigh above the carnage, twisting it tight with a stick and tied it off. The pain lanced through the shock and he put a second stick between his teeth so he wouldn't grind them to bits. Caleb thrust the wide blade of his largest knife into the coals of the smoldering fire.

He pulled out his sharpest skinning knife and without hesitation sliced through skin and muscle to separate his left knee joint.

He tried to scream past the stick as he worked, finally accepting the pain as the world he lived in while finishing the job. The smashed and splintered limb fell away. Caleb rolled over to the smoldering campfire embers, grabbed his large knife, and held it firmly against the bloody stump.

The stench of seared flesh saturated the air along with his scream of agony. Tears coursed down his face as he wrapped the stump in the cleanest piece of cloth he owned and tied it tight with rawhide lashings. Finally he crawled into the small tent and, despite threat from without, allowed himself unconsciousness.

Na'znn stirred from his comatose state and opened all senses to their widest spectrum. The familiar pilot nest of the scout craft invigorated his determination. He ingested sustenance from one of the combination of tubes at his side.

Energy surged through him and he directed the major portion to his brain. Fear still lurked in the edges of his mind and only a solution to his problem would banish it forever. *Why was the creature being so possessive of the fuel?*

If any void drives existed on this planet they were superior to the point they didn't emit the telling radiation inherent in the exhaust process. He doubted the technology necessary for construction of a sophisticated craft like his existed on this world. The fuel could not be ingested as sustenance by any living creature Na'znn had yet encountered, including the one with which he now vied.

This defied logic; what possible use could the creature have for soft metal of such dense complexity?

Na'znn ceased his thought processes. He was wasting precious time. When they established orbit around this planet all those cycles ago, they had investigated most of the non-liquid surface with their electronic probes.

They found many deposits of fuel, but this one lay closest to the surface and by far had the purest concentration of all, considering its bulk. He flushed his mind in exasperation. Of all the times to be challenged by a technically inferior race!

By his own count he had physically touched the surface of over a thousand different worlds. His name would forever be recited at the beginning of every new cycle as one of the Race's most prolific cosmic explorers. The Race had even named a distant star system for him. This voyage with a nubile female of great intelligence potential had been a reward unto itself.

The sex had been memorable. His mental glow chilled and splintered. Ta'ffil had been killed by a creature that, through its savage seizure and defense of valuable fuel, now threatened Na'znn's life as well.

His ship's disrupters were designed to eliminate herds of threats, not single ones. Nor did they discriminate between enemy and fuel. They disrupted all atoms completely and irrevocably. He would have to trap the creature away from the fuel, and kill it.

Caleb jerked in response to a dream, and the instant agony in his knee jerked him into howling consciousness. He dragged himself out into the light of a new dawn and pulled down the remnants of his breeches to examine the left thigh.

"No dark streaks," he grated, "…no pizen in the blood."

He ignored the pain thumping in tandem with his heart, taking stock of his situation. There was a critter from a man's sweatiest nightmares out there, and it wanted to kill him. It had damn near succeeded.

He chewed his pipe and wistfully dwelt on how much he would welcome a plug of real tobacco. Grinding his teeth on the stem, he realized he didn't have the luxury of thinking about anything other than how to kill that damned critter out there. It sure as hell wasn't going to let him haul the gold out of here without a fight.

What the hell would a thing like that want with gold? Did they deem the metal precious even in hell? After a moment's reflection, he decided there might be some currency in that notion after all.

How do you beat the devil, especially with only one leg?

The obvious hit him between the eyes like a Galena pill — you use the right bait!

Once he had the critter out of the way, Clark could carry him, or the gold, back to civilization. The animal couldn't bear both burdens.

Watching the sky and his surroundings constantly, using his Hawken as a staff, he hobbled around the area until he found a sapling with a gentle fork. With a few deft hatchet strokes and a rawhide lashing the sapling became a crutch complete with a beaver pelt pad for his armpit. After a few stumbles, he decided he needed a second crutch to allow him to move faster.

Within an hour he moved about the area smartly on two sticks. He fashioned a sling for the Hawken to hang across his back and practiced pulling the weapon around for instant presentation.

Using pain as a prod, he went about setting his trap.

Na'znn regained acuity before the preset alarm could wake him. Realizing he wasn't getting the amount of neural-cleansing unconsciousness his age and mass required gave him more pause and self-searching. Perhaps he should abandon this deposit and find another; alternative locations existed on this planet.

Unfortunately none so remote, the Divine Fruit alone knew what had happened on the alternate sites, assuming they still existed in the pristine state he and Ta'ffil had discovered so many cycles ago. He didn't like chance or ungoverned cilia.

Just how many cycles had passed on this planet? He relaxed his mind into computation mode, where he had always excelled since gaining cognizance. The answer surprised and subdued him instantly.

689 orbits around the planet's prime star had passed since he and his crewmate had stopped here to explore. Much could happen among these short-lived creatures in that amount of time. Such civilizations had been encountered before in the history of the Race and all had proved bothersome, unable to appreciate the future as species goal beyond their own immediate needs and desires.

Greedy. This creature is greedy, Na'znn realized with blinding clarity. *Offer it what it most desires.* Na'znn began checking the resources of his scout craft.

After a breakfast of roasted horsemeat, Caleb felt ready to fight. The morning sky held no clouds but a scent of newness in the air hinted at full spring, just a few weeks away. Another prod, Caleb thought. He didn't want to be in the mountains when the hostile tribes began stretching their legs.

Crutches were worthless in a running fight.

He finished loading the gold into the panniers on Clark. The horse was his best weapon. Clark could sense that rug from hell before Caleb even knew it was close. He rubbed the horse's bony skull between the upright ears.

"We get outta this one, old friend, and you'll never work again as long as you live. I'll feed you corn and fresh apples till you bust."

Clark swung his head around and regarded Caleb for a moment with one large, brown eye, and snorted in response.

Caleb missed Lewis, but the animal hadn't possessed half the brains Clark had. He hoped he could eventually find a woman with as much common sense as his horse. Abruptly he pushed those thoughts into the back of his mind, he didn't have time for daydreaming.

"C'mon, Clark, let's go bait the trap."

He looped Clark's reins through his leather belt and slung the Hawken on his back. He hated having to use both hands to ambulate; it just wasn't safe.

Slowly they traversed the meadow and stopped at a rock ledge that cupped slightly. A thick stand of fir grew on top of the ledge, offering concealment for his critter trap. Caleb took a deep breath and started climbing the gentle slope of the ridge. He knew this would be the hardest part. Clark followed, completely at ease.

Once they gained the top of the ridge, Caleb allowed himself a rest and some mouthfuls of water. Then he pulled his double-bladed axe out from its lashings atop the panniers and got to work.

Na'znn expelled a few densometers of fuel onto the planet surface, leaving only enough to return to the alpha ship. If he did not return with fuel, he would die in orbit around this backward planet, unsung and missed by few. He ejected himself from the scout craft without further consideration of his position, fearing he would not be at his warrior best.

For this expedition he wore both his personal nulgrav and his material-handler. If called to do so, he could lift a mass twice the size of the alpha ship in this gravity. The neural net he brought with was powered high enough to render unconsciousness to any species known to the Race.

He was angry beyond the dictates of good breeding and more than ready to rid himself of an inferior creature who had thus far thwarted him by pure chance. In moments he moved forward to where the fuel lay on the planet's surface. It did have a certain alluring sheen in its purest state, he decided, receptors firmly focused on visual.

The creature's vision, he had analyzed and decided, used only a third of the visual spectra available to the Race. Therefore he reduced his visual awareness to the same spectrum. Since he had such a technological advantage, he felt it worthy to at least narrow the conflict to the same spectra.

He attached the fuel to his material-handler and moved out to create his deception. The Race depended on him.

Caleb pushed the last boulder up the rough ramp and groaned when it fell onto the others. He wiped his brow and considered the prospect of defeat. Once he placed the counter-weight, how on earth would he release the force holding it in check?

He eyed the trees around him and spied two prospective allies in exactly the correct position. He grinned. More work, but now he knew his trap would work.

With a groan he rolled off the log and crutched over to an even larger rock. Half the day elapsed before Caleb finished his labors. Worried that it seemed obvious to the casual passerby, he cut more disguising fronds than he really needed.

He was ready for the critter.

Na'znn regarded his work and deemed it convincing. The amount of fuel used to lure the creature was small enough that if destroyed he wouldn't jeopardize his journey home. He engaged both his personal nulgrav and the material handler. They worked together as designed, lifting him quickly into the nitrogen-rich atmosphere.

Despite the indigenous creatures, this planet invigorated him to the point he felt multiples of cycles younger than his span. The thought gave him pause and a flicker of regret. This creature was obviously the dominant species on this planet. If they could be found in this remote location, they probably swarmed the rest of the landmasses.

The Laws of Exploration forbade displacing any species evolved sufficiently to the point of tool making. Na'znn doubted the creature he faced had created the primitive weapons he used so skillfully. Lost in his negative contemplation of his situation, he missed the lure on his first pass over the area.

The entire clutch of fuel the creature had appropriated lay in a pile at the base of a mineral up-thrust, directly in front of an impenetrable mass of the large celluloid stalks prevalent in this area. Na'znn powered down and anchored to a lateral juncture of the tallest stalk with a clear view of the clutch. Based on recent experience, something suspect hid in this situation.

It was everything he wanted on this planet.

The adversary creature was remote to the point that Na'znn's heat signature indicator detected nothing larger than the small cilia-covered warm-bloods that hopped around seemingly unaware of and constantly falling prey to larger warm-bloods or the variety of swift sky-creatures.

It had to be a trap.

How? He heightened his visual acuity to the maximum and carefully surveyed the areas above, and around the clutch. Nothing registered, nothing of importance moved. Keeping his first impulse firmly in mind, he moved to the second.

Could it be a gesture of acquiescence? He felt quite negative about that postulant. Had the creature become incapacitated?

Na'znn felt a charge of elation course through his body. *Of course, that was it!* He thought back to his attack; had he seen the piece of waste mineral actually hit the planet?

No.

Had he actually hit his target despite his equipment failure and the extraordinary senses of the beta animal? He wasn't sure. He could bite himself for leaving the scene before the attack reached total conclusion.

Doubt lead to conjecture and he finally decided that this could actually be a gesture of, if not surrender, perhaps truce. If true, he could go home, immediately. Na'znn played his detection equipment over the area one more time, and found naught.

At full alert, and with all senses wide open, he settled next to the clutch.

Caleb nearly fainted when the critter landed next to the gold.

The sonuvabitch actually took the bait! But it just sat there next to the pile. It needed to crawl up on it, so his aim would be perfect.

He didn't want to use his entire arsenal, it would mean a lot more work for him, and summer was coming fast.

The critter fluttered, or something, and it was on the close side of the pile. He wished he'd had the forethought to cock his Hawken. From here he could drill it clean and save everybody a mess of trouble.

However he knew the softest movement of metal on metal would spook that thing worse than shaking a Sioux rattle in a wild colt's face. Therefore he waited, knife bared and resting on the rope of horsehide crafted earlier. The horsehide not being cured even a little, stretched constantly with little groaning sounds, and he wondered how well, exactly, that critter could hear.

The critter did something and suddenly half the leather bags holding the gold just went away like ice melting. A hum filled the air and a line of gold suddenly shot through the air like a rope and the pile began to shrink down.

Hidden in the den he had dug out in the soil over the rock face, Caleb, without thinking, cocked the Hawken and aimed down at the device the critter had lit off. He fired and hit the thing dead center, blowing it into pieces.

"How many of them damn things does that critter have?"

Without hesitation he grabbed his knife, reached up and severed the horsehide rope. He pulled back into hole, knowing he had shot his bolt and if it didn't work, he was a goner.

Na'znn abruptly sequenced into attack mode when the molecular transfer node exploded. The roar of the chemical projectile came from above and he fired his disrupter at the source, activating the material handler at the same time to create a stasis field over the fuel clutch.

He started to lift off with the entire mass when the rock face above him roared down, burying him with the fuel.

"Damn, damn, damn!" Caleb screamed.

This wasn't what he had planned. That damn critter had botched everything. He pulled himself out of his little den and made his way down to the pile of rubble covering his gold.

Whatever that critter had shot at him must powerful poison. The blast had dislodged rocks three times the weight of Clark. There was no chance of Caleb digging the gold out by himself.

He eyed the thumb-thick line of gold heading ruler-straight toward the woods on the other side of the meadow. Getting Clark from his hiding place took longer than he liked, but his stump ached; his leg wanted rest.

The sun hung directly overhead by the time Caleb started picking up the gold. It had broken in many places but he still could find lengths up to a yard long. They were wonderfully heavy.

As he picked the metal off the ground, he loaded the two panniers on Clark at an even rate, so as not to throw the animal off balance. The gold stopped about fifty feet shy of the tree line. That critter's contraption would make a wonderful miner, Caleb decided.

The gold was completely pure; the humming thing had rejected any waste rock that might have stuck to it. After picking up the last of the gold, Caleb sat on one of the many large boulders in the meadow. He had enough to set himself up in St. Louis or perhaps somewhere smaller.

He'd always liked St. Genevieve just downriver from St. Louis. Real smart little town and the folks were friendly. Lots of pretty girls lived there, too, if memory served. A cloud had moved over the sun and when it passed something glinted in the grass near the tree line where the gold had been headed.

Caleb slowly looked all around the area before pushing himself upright, grunting a little with the bite of new pain. After adjusting the Hawken he crutched slowly toward the glint. He stopped and looked around again before staring down in disbelief.

More of the pure gold law scattered about like a load of firewood dropped after stumbling. The critter had to have put it there, but why? As bait, sure as winter snow.

It had planned to trap him! Caleb laughed out loud for a minute before remembering there might be other threats nearby. But this threat was buried under a ton of rocks; he knew that for fact.

Still he waited while he parsed it all out. The critter was the trapper, not the trap. Look as he might Caleb couldn't see any waiting jawed in the grass.

However that thing could fly, and might have traps that he couldn't even understand, let alone see. He had enough gold to buy land, build a house and probably purchase a successful business. Owning a mill had always appealed to him, folks always need the service of a good miller.

He didn't need that gold laying there, but it would sure as hell make a welcome addition to a man's old age. Something kept him from moving, something he couldn't put his finger on nagged at the back of his mind.

"Follow yer gut," Caleb said to himself.

He felt itchy, like the time he and Frenchy Joe found the burnt trapper cabin up in the Tetons. Caleb had counseled taking a different trail. Frenchy Joe insisted on continuing their direction and they stumbled into the midst of a Blackfoot war party.

Four of the nine Blackfoot had perished along with Frenchy Joe, and Caleb had high tailed out of there with an arrow through the thigh. He'd been double lucky that day; the arrow had missed the big artery in his leg. The old wound still troubled him when the weather changed.

Now he stared at the gold as dispassionately as he was able. He wondered what sort of trap a critter like that had in his outfit. He remembered the explosion after he killed the first critter, and wondered why there hadn't been an explosion after the second one was buried by a ton of rock.

Part of the trap, maybe?

What would it take to spring the trap, closer inspection? He was too far from the gold to reach it with his crutch. He needed a curved piece on the end of a pole.

After placing a piece of fringe from his coat on the ground to mark his closest advance, Caleb crutched backward away from the gold, worried something might charge out of the woods at him. Nothing moved. He glanced around at the saplings and found one that suited to perfection.

After another hard look around his horizon, he pulled his hatchet free and with a few economical strokes, converted the sapling into a two-pronged rake. He tied Clark to another sapling to keep him out of the way if somehow he tripped a trigger.

Clutching the rake and his crutch in his right hand was cumbersome and a bit painful, but possible.

He advanced to where the fringe lay on the ground. Raking four pieces of the gold over to where he stood proved simple. Another nine lay farther away. For the life of him he just couldn't see any trap.

"But neither does the beaver," he muttered to himself in a grim tone.

He shifted his left crutch and the arrow hit it instead of piercing through his side and into his heart.

"Damn! The Blackfoot found my trail." He threw himself to the ground behind one of the boulders as a small flurry of arrows whisked through space he had just vacated.

He pulled his Hawken around and cocked it. Resting it on the rock he pulled his heavy horse pistol out of his belt and cocked it as well. Somehow the pain in his leg didn't seem as intense as it had just moments ago.

He wished he'd had the presence of mind to count the arrows, but he knew he faced at least six warriors, maybe more. He glanced down at the shaft that had gone so far into the two-inch-thick crutch that the point of the arrow showed on the other side.

"One 'a them bastards out there's got a strong arm fer certain."

He forced himself silent. One of the bad habits a loner develops is talking out loud. Nervous as he might be, he had to keep his mouth shut. It was a pure wonder they couldn't hear his heart thudding in his chest.

It's been long enough, he thought, the one most excited about making a name for himself is going to do something brave, and stupid—

"Ei-yi-yi-yi!" the scream shot across the meadow ahead of the racing warrior. Caleb watched him for a long moment, admiring the physical sleekness of the young man, probably not twenty summers yet, as his greased muscles rippled and moved in a sinuous concert of power and agility. The warrior wore yellow and vermilion paint on his face, and some sort of bird and feather arrangement flopped in his knotted hair.

The brave waved a steel bladed hatchet in one hand and a fearsome war club in the other.

Caleb laid the Hawken down and picked up the horse pistol. When the screaming Blackfoot got within ten feet, Caleb shot him through the head. The ball hit him mid stride and dropped him flat on his back.

For a few moments the feet kept trying to run, drumming heels in the grass, and then stopped. Caleb had already reloaded the pistol. He twisted around, trying to look everywhere at once.

Another one or two would come at him from a different direction and the rest from a third compass point. Even if he had two legs this would be a bad spot. He figured he wouldn't have to worry about the gold any longer. "Dead men cain't spend," he whispered.

Running feet! There, behind him. They were between him and Clark now, grinning as they ran, proud owners of a new horse and a full season's pelts. Neither carried a firearm, both bore long handled, deadly steel hatchets traded from the French.

Caleb pulled both his knives free of their sheaths. Holding the big one in his left hand, he flipped the smaller one in his right and grasped it by the front of the blade, then threw. He sank the little knife into the closest brave's chest from twenty paces.

The second attacker glanced at his dying friend, and checked his rush maybe a half step, before throwing his enraged self at the *washicu*. Caleb parried the hatchet swing with his hastily grabbed right crutch and, holding his big knife blade downward and edge out, swung out and severed the second warrior's throat.

Panting, he threw himself to the ground before his adversary had time to stumble forward and fall. Three arrows whizzed over him. He lay on the ground longer than he dared, but he was completely winded and covered with sweat.

I'm too old for this life. Mebbe I stayed one season too long, but this was the season of the gold, he reflected.

Were only three left, maybe four? I might get out of this after all.

Shrieks filled the air and he twisted around to see five Blackfoot charging from the other side of the tree line straight at him. Earlier he had figured the dead critter's trap zone was at least a fifty-foot circle and he knew it was close to the gold bait. They were going to run right through it!

One of the Blackfoot had a Pennsylvania rifle and pulled up short to shoot at Caleb. The ball took Caleb's left ear lobe off and pissed him mightily.

"Yew bastard!" He leveled the Hawken and shot the Indian through the chest. The man spun and dropped.

The other four shrieked all the louder, knowing Caleb didn't have time to reload, and that they had him outnumbered—

A piercing, unearthly, *gleet* rang out from the denser woods. The two braves closest to the sound slowed and turned their attention to a possible new threat. The other two continued their shrieking attack — and suddenly blew to bits as a high-pitched, jaw-aching sound issued from the woods.

Caleb's jaw dropped open as he tried to see pieces of the two men or their weapons. The just weren't there any more! The remaining two Indians stared at Caleb in astonishment, glanced at each other, then turned and fled in the other direction.

At any other time Caleb would have hugely enjoyed the obvious misconstruction of the situation by the Blackfoot. However he was still trying to find some evidence that the other two braves had ever existed. There wasn't even a feather left.

He stood and looked down at the gold on the ground. Pursing his lips, he nodded toward the gold and whatever else was back there, and turned to collect his weapons. He took one step and halted in astonishment.

A small mountain sailed through the air, directly at him. The instant realization that he had underestimated the critter didn't give him pause. That thing had just saved his bacon and no mistake, whether it did it on purpose or not.

A fierce kinship bloomed in him, and he cheered as rock and dirt tumbled to the ground and the critter flew over him with the bait gold.

When the rock face fell on him, a large piece of stone had hit Na'znn's core lump and knocked him into a comatose state. After some degrees of the planet's revolution, he collected his synapses and surveyed his situation. The material handler held its field effortlessly and Na'znn thanked the Divine Fruit for the solid technical expertise of the Race.

He heard the defense perimeter sound its warning and then the disrupter fire. The creature had taken his bait! Na'znn rippled instructions into the material lifter and his personal nulgrav, then he and the mass of waste rock above him lifted into the air.

With a deft twitch he rocked the material lifter to the side and the mass of waste material smashed to the planet surface. Carrying only the clutch of precious fuel, he set course for his scout ship.

Abruptly he felt complete bewilderment when he flew directly over the equally astonished creature. He settled over the ship and instantly fed the fuel into the sorter maw. He rotated in the atmosphere and looked back at the creature.

He could leave now; he had enough fuel to make it to the next star system where two planets held impressive amounts of fuel. However would this creature contest his acquisition of the fuel it held in such high regard?

It finally moved. Holding its chemical weapon above its body, it raised and lowered the weapon in two quick jerks. Then it turned and juttered away. One of its lower limbs had been lost. Na'znn allowed a touch of smugness to cloud his mind before diving into the scout craft. His trajectory had been perfect but for the chemical projectile offsetting it a mere fraction of a multiple.

He slid into the pilot's perch and activated the ship.

The farther Caleb got from the situation, the less he believed what he had witnessed. However two panniers stuffed with gold validated all his recollections, no matter how strange.

"It went straight up into the air, clear out of sight! You saw it, Clark, didn't ya?"

The horse swung its head to the left enough to acknowledge the question and then faced forward as the two slowly moved east, out of the mountains, and toward St. Genevieve.

Diplomatic Exchange

THIS WAS *NOT* THE PHILADELPHIA WHERE THEY HAD LUNCH...

FROM THE AUTHOR OF WHALESONG

STONEY COMPTON

My good friend, Paul Sherry, gave me the brain bug for this story. Being a history freak I did a lot of research on the era and the events surrounding the Constitutional Convention (which started out as the Convention to Amend the Articles of Confederation). The best work that describes the events is *Miracle at Philadelphia* by Catherine Dinker Bowen, a book I highly recommend for every American.

Diplomatic Exchange

1
Philadelphia - May, 2019

Nick Gordon pushed a fader switch across his control board, and peered at the cluster of read-outs and digital gauges recessed into the metal. "Dammit! It's not closing, Annie." He licked his lips and pushed errant hairs away from his eyes.

"But it should be! If you rerouted the subroutine when we added the—"

"The bridge protocol," Nick said with a groan. "Jeeze. Of course, I spaced it."

Annie Malone looked away, grinding her teeth. "I told you twice..." She double-clicked on a file, did it again. "Okay, it's reloaded. Now try it."

She tried to hold her temper but, dammit, he was the physics graduate student, not her. She was here to record the historical results - if any.

Nick again nudged the control. A low hum filled the air. The read-outs flickered, registering massive electro-magnetic loads. Nick and Annie stared beyond the bank of computers and junction boxes to the middle of the large room.

Ozone permeated the air. Light metal mesh enclosing a sixty by forty foot section of the floor space glowed, emitting a faint blue haze. Annie thought it resembled a huge block of electric ice.

"It's holding. My God, Annie, we've achieved a static field."

"Dr. Mason isn't going to believe this," she said, her anger instantly dissipating. "And I've got call Ruth immediately. She'll need the time to make all her reality checks."

"Must be great having an advisor who doesn't think you're nuts," Nick said.

"We're just lucky that Mason can't kill the project." She squeezed his shoulder, pretending not to notice when he leaned into the pressure. She pulled her hand away. "Guess I'd better start making phone calls."

"Yeah." Nick watched her move into the small office and pick up the phone. *She had everything,* he thought. *Beauty, brains, and a militant boyfriend who wasn't smart enough to handle a 200 level physics course.*

He sighed and powered down the system. Best keep his mind on the project. Tonight would be the first formal test.

"Ruth," Annie said.

"Yeah?"

"Did I wake you?"

"Yeah," said the sleepy voice, "and you better have a damn good reason."

"The field holds. You're the first one I called."

"I'll be there by 5:30."

Annie disconnected, pushed another button.

"Dr. Mason?"

"This is Mason," the nasal voice snapped. "Make it quick."

"This is Annie Malone. I suggest you postpone any plans for this evening."

"I told you, no more meetings until you can produce verifiable results."

"Our first field test is tonight at seven," she said, keeping her words crisp. "Doctor Frank and General Waverly will both be present." She crossed her fingers, watching Nick through the glass wall. She wondered how he put up with this man.

"If I don't see evidence of success, Mr. Gordon can start rewriting his thesis."

"Excuse me, Dr. Mason, we have a lot to do before seven. I hope you can make it." She hung up. *To hell with you,* she thought, *not even you can keep Nick from getting his doctorate now.*

Her advisor, Dr. Frank, waxed enthusiastic. He promised to be early. She smiled, punching in General Waverly's number.

"Colonel Thiebaldt speaking." Annie grimaced at the pomposity that flooded the connection.

"Good afternoon, Colonel. This is Annie Malone. Could I speak to General Waverly please?"

"May I tell him the nature of your call, Miss Malone?"

"Certainly! It's classified."

"Very well." She felt the frost over the line and smiled.

"Waverly here," his deep voice brought his sturdy African-American figure to her mind. She smiled.

"Hi, it's Annie. The balloon goes up at seven tonight. Can you be here?"

"Ha. Try and keep me away. Would you be free for dinner after?"

"I'm already tired, General. But I'd love it if you'd bring me some Chinese take-out, bring enough for Nick, too. Okay?"

"I certainly opened myself up for that one," Waverly said genially. "Okay, dinner's on me."

Annie skipped back into the lab. "They're all coming, Nick! We're really going to do it."

He smiled up at her. "We're really going to try it. Hand me that magnometer, would you? Jeeze, I'm starving."

"You're not going to eat it are you?"

2

Philadelphia - May 13, 1787

The impeccably maintained coach and four came to a halt on the cobblestones in front of a well-kept brick house. Even though summer was officially a month away, the day hung heavy with moist heat and the noisome odors of crowded civilization. A tall, broad-shouldered man stepped down from the carriage and nodded to the driver who clucked his team into a walk on down the street.

The carriage passed a stick-wielding man who, with the aid of a dog, herded a small flock of geese toward the market. Another man pushed a rude wheelbarrow holding a tightly trussed hog that grunted at every bump on the uneven cobbles.

As the man neared the house, a handsome woman in her thirties opened the heavy door and curtsied. Her clothes conveyed sensibility without total accommodation to thrift.

"Welcome, General Washington. Won't you please come in? I'll advise Dr. Franklin of your arrival."

"Thank you, Mrs. Connor." George Washington gave her a tight smile and removing his tricorner, laid it on the bench next to the door while mopping his brow with a lace kerchief.

Benjamin Franklin limped into the room and stopped, made a small bow. His stomach bulged through his unbuttoned waistcoat.

"You honor my home with your presence, General."

"An invitation to dine with the witty Doctor Franklin is the highest honor this city can hope to bestow." Washington glanced about. "Has Mr. Madison arrived yet?"

"Indeed. He is sampling my latest shipment of porter. Please, come join us. Mrs. Connor will have dinner for us anon."

"Her cooking," Washington said with a smile, "accounts for a good part of the high esteem this house enjoys."

"I *am* blessed." Franklin nodded.

The two men ambled into the parlor where James Madison sat staring at a tankard of dark porter. He glanced up, and then scrambled to his feet.

"General Washington! How good to see you, sir."

Washington smiled at Madison. Both Washington and Franklin towered over Madison.

"One would believe you hadn't seen me just hours ago at the State House." They both made slight bows.

"Ah," Madison said, "but that was the people's business. This, sir, is personal pleasure."

"You do realize, sir," Washington said to Franklin with a nod toward Madison. "It is a rare case indeed, when one's political associate becomes a personal friend."

"We all speak as friends here this evening, even though we must speak of those who are not," Franklin said with a brief frown. "But first, please give us your judgment on this excellent porter, General. It's some of England's finest."

Washington poured himself a tankard from the small cask at table edge. He held the tankard in front of his face, sniffed. "It has a good nose." He took a sip, wiped foam from the edges of his mouth, finally swallowed. "Somewhat fruity which adds to the robust body. A good batch, Doctor Franklin." He took another swallow before setting the tankard down.

Smiling, Franklin held no doubt that at the end of the evening General Washington will have outdrank his companions and suffer naught the evening. The general enjoyed his spirits and distilled some of the finest whiskey in Virginia.

"I appreciate the solace this house offers," Washington said. "Out there," he nodded toward the street, "reigns discord and strife, pushed by ambition without thought beyond immediate gratification."

Madison's voice sounded as fife to Washington's drum. "Distrust has become the unifying bond between the states, in all else agreement goes wanting."

"Despite our noble ally, Mr. Hamilton," Franklin said, "the other New York delegates promise to forestall any attempts at a strong central government. I have the latest papers from that place wherein Governor Clinton preaches his cacophony of doom and predictions of the states enslaved by a new monarchy."

Washington's countenance went bleak and cold.

"Yes, he would rather see us a band of squabbling, fractious demi-nations able to do naught in concert. He cannot see that we are at the mercy of foreign powers who would manipulate us as thirteen puppets."

"Perhaps there will be but twelve states with a strong central government," Madison said.

"With New York dividing that nation in half? It would not do, sir," Washington said.

"I remind you, gentlemen," Madison said with a grim smile,

"Mr. Hamilton has already taken a house here in Philadelphia, and will swell our ranks."

Mrs. Connor entered the room. "Doctor Franklin, gentlemen, dinner is served."

Franklin caught the quickness in Washington's step as he followed Mrs. Connor. His appetite for spirits was completely eclipsed when it came to victuals. Limping after his guests, Benjamin Franklin thought this would be an evening to remember, despite his pesky gout.

3

Philadelphia - 2019

Dr. Frank raised his voice slightly, "Although the combat portion of the Revolution was over. British troops were still entrenched on U. S. soil. French agents were constantly meddling in national affairs, trying to make us a vassal state. Half the populace feared a strong government which a constitutional convention would surely produce."

"I'm sure we have the picture, Doctor," Dr. Mason said firmly. "Can we get on with this farce?"

Dr. Frank nodded at Annie.

"Please turn off all cell phones. They won't work in here due to the electromagnetic shielding and they play havoc with our electronics. Thank you.

"I am switching on the cameras," Annie said in her official voice. She pushed the RECORD button on her console while glancing at all four cameras to check their glowing red function lights. "This is the first field test of the Project Gernsback Temporal Information Array."

"The array is closing," Nick said tightly. "Boost the power gain, Ruth."

"Mind your own board, dearie," Dr. Ruth Hampstead slowly twisted the dial to a higher setting, "...and the rest of us will do our part."

Despite the air conditioning, Annie felt a bead of sweat creeping down her left temple. The room-circling silver band constituting the array gave off a slight crackle and began to emit a faint blue glow. Ozone tickled her nose.

"General Waverly, would you please turn out the overhead lights?" Dr. Mason said without taking his eyes off Nick's monitor.

Annie anxiously watched the General as he negotiated the equipment-filled space outside the array, her eyes flicked from person to person, anything to avoid watching the array for a moment. She unsuccessfully tried to relax.

Dr. Frank, her advisor, sat on the edge of his folding chair, staring intently at the mesh. A hum slowly swelled along with the intensity of the blue glow. Annie possessed a basic understanding of the computer protocols of the interface, however the physics portion of Project Gernsback eluded her.

She and Dr. Frank were there to interpret what they saw and

heard. If the Temporal Information Array actually provided a window into the past the observed results would be the meat of her doctoral dissertation.

General Waverly carefully eased past her and settled into his chair. "How long will it take to come up to full power?"

"Don't know for sure," Nick said absently, keying commands into the computer. "But in theory not more than a minute or two. This is a field test, we've never cranked the grid up to full power before."

Annie checked the digital readout, silently measuring the first minute's passage. She leaned back in her chair and closed her eyes. Two years of hard work would bear fruit in the next few minutes — or lengthen into yet more temporal mechanics and cobbled equipment — even if Dr. Mason assented.

Good thing we have some government R&D money to bolster the Gernsback grant, she thought.

The hum sharpened to a whine. Tiny sparkles danced across the mesh, leaving minute holes in the blue sheen that immediately snapped closed. Nick frowned at the array and nudged a fader switch.

The glow suddenly flashed up to the ceiling-mounted grid boundaries, hesitating for a nanosecond before rippling together with a crackle. The array resembled an electric, transparent tarp around a huge block of ice.

"It's up," Dr. Mason said. "And it's holding!"

Nick's fingers flew over the keyboard. The whine eased and the blue ebbed to transparency as a scene slowly solidified inside the array.

Three men sat around a polished wooden table covered with the remains of a rather large meal. As if emerging from a mist, the features of the men became distinct.

Annie gasped in recognition as Dr. Benjamin Franklin raised a glass and clearly intoned, "To a truly United States, gentlemen. May our labors bear republic fruit."

General George Washington raised his glass, mirroring the action of James Madison who said, "Hear him, hear him."

The three men drank.

Annie glanced around at the other team members. General Waverly, the whites of his eyes contrasting with his shadowed, dark features, stared in wonder, his jovial skepticism dying once and for all.

Dr. Ruth Hampstead wore a beatific smile as her eyes flicked from readouts to the array and back. Nick sat with hands poised over the keyboard, his eyes all but bugging out. Warm affection flowed through Annie as she smiled at her genius partner.

Dr. Frank put his hand on hers and squeezed. "We're exactly on target," he whispered tensely. "Are we getting everything?"

She pulled her hand away and pushed the monitor display. "Three minutes plus, and running," she whispered back.

"Colonel Thiebaldt approached me today as I left the State House," George Washington said to his companions, "and urged me to seize power from the congress and convention. 'The Society of the Cincinnati will back you as monarch,' the rascal said. As if I had not refused the same offer from Congress four years ago."

Nick and Annie stared at each other. Nick silently mouthed, Thiebaldt?

She shrugged theatrically.

"He hungers for power, that one," Madison said. "He may have been an officer, but never will he enjoy the title of gentleman from my lips."

"'Tis only human nature," the portly Franklin said with a chuckle, "to attempt filling a powerful seat freshly vacated. I have heard it bandied about that some of these former officers would see themselves as the new American nobility."

"Precisely," Washington said with a snort. "I advised Mr. Thiebaldt to find another avenue in which to serve his country, or attempt commerce and put his zeal to fiduciary use."

"Do you feel they will pressure you further?" Madison asked in his high, thin voice.

Outside the array, Dr. Frank eased out of his chair and drew closer to the perimeter of the energy field, his body tense and his face rapt. Dr. Mason frowned and moved carefully over to the older man. His action put him directly in front of General Waverly, who tugged at his sleeve.

"What is the Society of the Cincinnati?" he whispered.

Mason leaned down to the General's ear. "Ask the historian, here." He nodded toward Annie.

The General leaned his head toward her.

"Ex-Revolutionary War officers, rather like the VFW or American Legion," she whispered. "Conservative to the point of being Royalists. They held a convention in Philadelphia at the same time the Constitutional Convention was in session.

Washington actually went into hiding to avoid them."

"They wanted him to be king?" he hissed.

"Some of them, general. And they wanted to be the American House of Lords."

Waverly glanced up to find both academics blocking his view. The General eased to his feet and stood beside the men.

"We would be hard pressed to dissuade them," Washington said.

"Perhaps you should avoid them like the pox," Franklin said with a wheezy chuckle.

"Is there any other cure you could recommend, Doctor?" Washington asked with a wry smile.

"Don't touch the field!" Nick hissed, urgency in his voice.

Annie glanced at the three men standing beside her. Dr. Frank, renowned expert on the Early Federalist Period, stood mesmerized by the spectacle in front of him. This was much more than any of the faculty had anticipated and Annie knew his mind ranged far from practical matters, such as the need to exercise caution.

She reached up to pull him back.

Dr. Mason twisted and whispered something to General Waverly. The array sparkled randomly with tiny blue flashes, using petawatts of power to maintain the window between the centuries.

Annie's hand had closed to within a few centimeters of Dr. Frank's hand when a blue spark arced between them. Dr. Frank gasped in surprise and jerked away from the tiny electrical bite. His shoulder hit Dr. Mason who lost his balance and started to fall forward.

General Waverly clutched at Mason. "Look out!"

The three men were suddenly bathed from head to foot in an actinic blue glow. With a loud "pop" the array vanished and the circuit breakers tripped with a bang. The lights and electronic equipment went dark.

"God damn it!" Nick shrieked. "This could take days to fix!"

"Quit bitching and reset the breakers," Ruth snapped.

Annie's eyes adjusted to the darkness and she could see the figures of the three men in front of her slowly get to their feet.

"Are you okay, Dr. Frank? Dr. Mason? General Waverly?" Annie asked.

The overhead lights blazed on.

Annie said, "Oh, my God."

Dr. Benjamin Franklin looked at her with wide eyes, then said to George Washington, "This is a good portent, she thinks *we* are the deity."

4

Philadelphia - 1787

General Waverly pushed the history professor off of him. "My God, man, your clumsiness has ruined this project!"

Dr. Frank grunted to his feet and looked around. "I don't think we're in Kansas any more, Toto."

Dr. Mason stared at the room while allowing the General to help him up. The substantial table and its remains mocked him. Wide eyed, he peered about the room, searching for the equipment or the rest of their team. The heavy aroma of roast beef and the scent of candle wax caught at his nose. "Oh, my word," he whispered. "This just can't be."

Footsteps sounded from a doorway now visible to them.

"Dr. Franklin, I heard a commotion," a woman's voice said. "Is something amiss?"

All three men looked wildly about them, seeking escape and finding none. An attractive middle-aged woman appeared in the door, her light gray dress buttoned snugly around her neck, while the hem of her skirt nearly touched the carpeted floor. Her smile of anticipation vanished when she saw them, and her eyes grew round.

"Wh-who are you?" What have you done with Dr. Franklin and his guests?" She pulled back into the small hallway as if to flee.

"Good lady," Dr. Frank said quickly. "I'm afraid there has been a very unique accident..."

"Pray thee, sir, explain it quickly or I summon the constable."

"You are aware that Dr. Franklin pursues scientific experiments?"

"Of course, but rarely in the dining room." Her manner grew visibly steadier. "I have been in his service for over five years. How does his work explain his absence and your presence? And what manner of dress is this?"

"Both the good doctor and we," Frank gestured toward his companions, "were conducting an experiment in communication," he licked his lips, "and something went horribly awry."

"Awry?" She glanced at the other two for a moment, lingering longest on General Waverly, before again fixing her gaze on Dr. Frank.

"I'm afraid that we three have inadvertently traded places with

Dr. Franklin, General Washington, and Mr. Madison." Dr. Frank let his voice trail away as a feeling of admiration for this sturdy woman swept over him.

"And exactly where, sir, is your place?"

"I'm afraid it's more *when* than *where*."

"Sir?" Her lower lip trembled.

Dr. Frank swallowed and glanced at the others. Both men appeared to be in as much shock as the woman. He looked at her and as gently as possible said, "We are from your future."

"Future," she echoed, wide eyes searching his face.

"2019 to be exact."

Her eyes rolled back in her head and, had he not rushed forward and caught her, she would have fallen face down on the floor.

"My God," Mason said thickly. "I feel faint, myself."

"Where are Franklin, Washington, and Madison?" General Waverly asked, peering around the room.

"It's my guess," Mason said, dropping into an upholstered chair, "they're through the looking glass and squarely in the third millennium."

"Can we reverse this?" the General demanded.

"We can't do a damned thing." Mason's voice sounded bitter. "Other than hope that young, pre-doctoral, Nicholas Gordon can work a miracle."

"Hand me that wine, or whatever it is," Dr. Frank said, leaning over the fallen woman.

General Waverly sniffed the half filled tankard and handed it to his colleague. "I think it's some sort of beer."

Dr. Frank cradled the woman's head in one arm and tipped the tankard to her lips. She swallowed, coughed, and her eyes fluttered open.

"I'm afraid we are still here, madam. Please be assured we mean you no harm and would immediately reverse the situation if it were in our power to do so."

"I am not afraid of you, sir," she said firmly as he helped her to her feet. She glanced past him, brushing at her dress. "Were I not mistaken, it would seem you three are afraid of me."

"Enchanted perhaps, madam," General Waverly said with a wide smile. "But never frightened."

He introduced himself and the other two men to her. "We listened to a few minutes of conversation in this room before our unfortunate accident occurred. But we did not hear your name."

"Pleased to meet you, gentlemen. I am Mrs. Conner, Dr. Franklin's housekeeper."

Pounding erupted at the front door.

"My word," said Mrs. Conner. "Someone is quite rude."

"Open the door in the name of the Society of the Cincinnati!" came a shout. "Or we'll break it in!"

General George Washington edged slightly ahead of Dr. Franklin, using his left arm to push James Madison behind him. His gray eyes flashing, he glanced around the room, hesitating on the profusion of equipment before fastening his gaze on Nick Gordon.

"If this is a scheme to do us injury, be assured, we will not submit willingly."

Annie stood up, attempting to overcome the incongruity of the situation. "We mean you no harm, gentlemen. In fact, it is due to the fascination and high regard in which we hold the three of you, that, ah, we inadvertently brought you here today."

She made introductions while taking in their physical differences. Washington stood a few inches taller than Franklin, Madison barely came up to his shoulder. Washington's strong features radiated authority, even though she thought his nose a bit large for the rest of his oval face. Prominent cheekbones added to his strong aura. For a 55 year-old man, George Washington seemed to be at the peak of his physical life.

Benjamin Franklin continued to stare around the room, eyes wide. "You mollify us somewhat, Miss Malone," he said, finally fixing his gaze on her. "But where, precisely, is here? And what manner of engines are these? And," he pointed up at the light bulbs, "how do you create illumination without making smoke? Have you perfected the capture of electric fluid?"

"Yes, we have indeed perfected the capture of electric fluid and have the means to create it as needed," Ruth said. "These engines," she gestured at the equipment, "are part of an experiment we were performing."

"Experiment?" Franklin said, eyebrows rising avidly.

"Yes, sir. This is our first attempt to look back through time."

Annie felt a kinship with the quick-witted man. Franklin's rapid adjustment to the scenario and his instant curiosity for everything he beheld, hinted at an agile mind.

In a low, nearly inaudible tone, James Madison said, "Look back through time? If we were the focus of your labors, you must represent our future, yes?"

"You are correct, Mr. Madison," Annie said.

"Where are we located on the calendar, then?" Franklin asked.

"At the beginning of the third millennium, 2019," Annie said, barely above a whisper.

"This is a ruse, a fantastic charade!" Washington said, his face clouding. "What you are saying is impossible."

"My good General," Franklin said, pointing up at the light bulbs. "Those are impossible, yet they seem to have a ready supply. By some strange machination we are no longer where we belong."

"We wanted to eavesdrop on you, gentlemen," Annie said. "We allotted great sums of money and massive amounts of energy in this attempt to peer back through time. We had a small mishap, and the experiment suddenly switched you three gentlemen with three of our people."

"Switched?" Franklin said.

"Yes. Three people from our time have vanished, you three have appeared." Annie said. "What would your assumption be?"

"That three people from the future are in my living room," Franklin said.

"I assure you, Dr. Franklin, all three are honorable men," Annie said.

"Why," Madison asked, "were you 'eavesdropping' on us?"

"The event you're embarking on, in 1787, changed the history of the world," she said.

"In what manner, young woman?" Madison asked.

"You created the first representative government on the planet. Look, we're playing with fire here."

"Fire?" Franklin said, craning his neck. "I see illumination but no fire."

"It's a figure of speech, sir. What I mean is, we've got to get you back to your own time. If you see, or hear, too much, it could influence you in some manner that might change history."

"Your world is so perfect that change might not enhance it?" Madison asked with a sniff.

Before Annie could form a response, the telephone rang. Ruth answered, held her hand over the receiver. "It's Colonel Thiebaldt. He wants to speak with General Waverly."

Nick took the phone. "Uh, Colonel Thiebaldt, General Waverly isn't able to come to the phone right now. No, sir. Colonel, he's… in the men's room." Nick grinned at the rest of them.

"Yes, we had an electrical overload and we're in the process of correcting the problem. Listen, Colonel, we're pretty busy right now and it looks like it's going to be a long night, I'll tell him you checked in. Yes, sir. Thank you."

Nick hung up the phone and rubbed his eyes.

"What is that instrument?" Franklin asked. "You were in communication with someone, were you not?"

"Time out," Annie said. "Gentlemen, please excuse us for a moment, but I must confer with my colleagues."

"I feel we three should be privy to any sort of conference which concerns us," Washington said.

"I concur," Madison said.

Dr. Ruth Hampstead raised her hand. "Okay, wait a minute. Annie, I think they're right. Whatever we say, we should say it in front of them."

"It's simply this," Annie said, "how much of our world can we show them? So far nothing has changed, that I know about, due to their presence. So we must have returned them to 1787 or things would be different."

Nick scratched his head. "Jeeze, this is like a weird science fiction novel. But Annie has a good point. If they don't get back for the convention when they're supposed to it will change something and we'll be responsible."

"But would we even know it?" Ruth asked. "If it changed then it would be common knowledge now, right?"

"This is an interesting conundrum," Franklin said with a wry smile. "But I venture to say that no matter what marvels you reveal to us, we will be able to keep our world and yours separate when, or if, we return."

"Where are we, geographically?" Washington asked.

"Philadelphia, Pennsylvania, United States of America," Annie said. "Some buildings still exist from your era. Your home, Dr. Franklin, and Independence Hall are the two most important."

"Independence Hall?" Madison echoed. "I know of no such structure."

"Sorry," Annie said, blushing. "You know it as the Pennsylvania State House."

"We still have the Liberty Bell, too," Nick said.

"Despite its shoddy workmanship?" Franklin asked with a grin.

"Yeah," Nick said. "We thought it was worth keeping."

"Is it within your power to return us to where we belong?"

Madison asked.

Annie looked across the room to where Ruth and Nick stood staring at the visitors. "Uh, yes, as soon as we figure out what happened. Guys?"

Nick and Ruth both guiltily stared down at their equipment.

Ruth glanced over at Nick. "Switch everything off and then reset the breakers."

"Right." Their hands moved swiftly over the consoles, staccato clicks echoed through the room. Nick reset the breakers and nodded at Ruth.

"Okay," she said. "Here goes nothing."

"What a curious comment," Franklin said in a low voice. "How can nothing go any where?"

Washington slowly surveyed everything and everybody in the room. "Miss Malone…"

"Yes, General Washington?" She suddenly grinned and shook her head. "My God, I can't get over the fact that I'm really talking to you."

"Nor I you," he replied. "When you spoke into that device," he pointed at the telephone, "you said a name. Would you please repeat that name?"

"I was speaking to Lt. Col. Thiebaldt. He is in charge of outside security for this project."

"Did he have an ancestor who served in the War of Independence?"

"I don't know, General Washington. Frankly I don't care for the man and therefore know very little about him, let alone his family. When you were dining at Doctor Franklin's, you mentioned the same name."

"Yes. I assume you also heard that I held the individual in low repute." Washington gave her a glacial smile. "Perhaps they are related."

"Our Thiebaldt is head of the military training component of this university. He was assigned to provide security for this project without being told of its nature." Annie stared into the close-walled distance. "I think it's making him crazy, not knowing what we're doing here. He seems driven-"

"The TIA bridge isn't responding," Ruth said. "Everything seems to be in place, but…"

"We're missing three sub-routines," Nick said.

"Three?" Annie said. "You must have lost a processor or a

motherboard."

"Processor. Motherboard. They speak nonsense here," Madison said to Franklin.

"I suspect, Mr. Madison," Franklin said while slowly limping toward the console, "...that a painted savage before the time of Columbus would find the terms, axle, harness, or coach equally arcane."

"Dr. Franklin is correct," Annie said. "They are nothing more than parts of a tool. Are you suffering from gout, Dr. Franklin?"

"Why, yes, I am. Do you have some magic to cure it?"

"We have pills that reduce swelling, and remove the uric acid in your blood, which is the cause of gout."

"Are you a physician, young woman?" Franklin asked.

"Gosh, no. My dad has gout, that's how I found out about it."

"How would I obtain some of these magical pills?"

"They're prescription only, but Dad left some at my house for when he visits."

"They've cured gout!" Franklin said to Madison. "I'm beginning to believe they can do anything."

"The motherboard is fried," Nick said with a moan. I'm going to have to build a new one."

"How long are we looking at?" Annie asked.

Nick yawned. "Well, if I can stay awake, between four and six hours, depends on what I have in the cabinet."

"You were here long before I was today," Ruth said. "Why don't you let me build a new one. You two show our guests some hospitality and get a little rest at the same time."

"Thanks, Ruth," Nick said, smiling. "I really appreciate that."

"Where are we going to take them?" Annie said. "Where can we take them?"

"Miss Malone," Franklin said.

"Annie."

"Very well. Miss Annie, we have already seen wonders beyond our comprehension. If, or when, you are successful in returning us to our own time..." he waved his hand, "...all of this will seem a fantastic dream. Pray, allow us the most grandiose dream possible."

The phone rang and Nick answered, "Hello." His gaze locked on Annie's. "No, Col. Thiebaldt, General Waverly isn't available... No. sir, I am not trying to pull anything, I... I'm sorry, Colonel, but this area is restricted–"

Nick slammed the phone down. "Damn! He's on his way over."

"But this is a restricted area," Annie said. "He can't just–"

"Yeah, that's what I tried to say," Nick said. "He told me I could try to stop him."

Annie turned toward the time travelers. "Gentlemen, we have to find some place to hide you, quickly."

"But isn't this person part of your organization?" Franklin asked.

"Well, yes," Annie said. "But–"

The door flew open and Lt. Colonel Harald Thiebaldt entered, flanked by two armed guards. "Okay, now I want to know what's going on around here."

"Migawd, the Society of the Cincinnati!" General Waverly said. "Isn't that the outfit we were talking about just before the accident?"

"Yes," Dr. Frank said, frowning. "But there is no record of them annoying Washington today."

"Perhaps history is an imperfect science?" Dr. Mason said. "How could you hope to know everything that happened on any particular day in the distant past?"

"Well, something of this magnitude–"

"Gentlemen," Gen. Waverly said forcefully. "We don't have time for–"

"Open this door!" The pounding intensified.

Mrs. Conner adjusted her sleeves while moving to the door and pulled it open. "Who do you think you are to be taking such liberties with Dr. Franklin's front door?" she blazed.

A knot of suddenly abashed men eddied backward. The leader quickly regained his composure. "With all due apologies, ma'am, but we're here to see General Washington, and we shall remain in this doorway until he speaks with us."

"General Washington is not here, Mr...."

"Colonel Thiebaldt. And I mean no disrespect, but we watched the general enter, and he has not left by any door or window of this house."

"I quite assure you, sir, General Washington is not on the premises."

Men in the group began muttering darkly.

"With or without you permission, ma'am, we'll see for ourselves." Thiebaldt pushed past her and entered the foyer. Seven men pushed through the door behind him.

General Waverly stretched to his full 6' 6" and glared down at them. "You are no gentlemen to besmirch an honest woman's word!"

The men jerked to a halt and stared up at him.

"A blackamoor!" Thiebaldt said. "In some manner of uniform."

"I am a general, Mr. Thiebaldt, and I demand that you take yourself and your friends out of this house at once!"

"What kind of uniform is that?" one of the men behind

Thiebaldt asked. "Never have I seen its like before."

"A general in what army?" Thiebaldt asked, edging back.

Dr. Frank tugged at the general's sleeve, whispered, "Don't say anything about the future, we could do irreparable harm."

Still glaring at Thiebaldt, Waverly considered Dr. Frank's words. At the same time he hid his amazement that the man in front of him looked identical to his adjutant over two centuries in the future. "I am a general in the Union Society, Mr. Thiebaldt, an ally of the United States."

"What form of government do you propose for the United States?" Thiebaldt asked.

"A representative form of government. Leaders voted into office by the people and responsible to them."

Theibaldt's glare darkened and his face grew mottled. "You're like the rest of the fools in this house. You would treat an officer the same as the lowest cook's apprentice!"

"Isn't that part of the reason we fought the War of Independence? Does not Mr. Jefferson's Declaration contain the passage; 'All men are created equal?'"

"Yes," Thiebaldt said with a smile. "But there are exceptions. For instance he did not include slaves and women in his declaration. Which begs the question; do you have manumission papers?"

"In my country all men are free and we don't need papers to prove it."

"Exactly where is your country, General?"

Mrs. Conner pushed in front of Thiebaldt. "These gentlemen are guests of Dr. Franklin. I don't care what service you performed in the war, it would not do to provoke Philadelphia's first citizen!"

"I'll have that from Dr. Franklin's lips, if you don't mind." Thiebaldt turned to his followers. "Take these strangers into custody. We'll get to the bottom of this puzzle sooner or later."

"I'll have the constable on you for this!" Mrs. Conner snapped.

"Very well, madam," Thiebaldt said, grabbing her arm. "Since you insist, we'll take you along, too."

Waverly glanced at his companions. He thought Dr. Mason looked pastier than usual, and Dr. Frank, although incensed, didn't have the physique for hand-to-hand combat. His only ally would be Mrs. Conner, who probably could overcome at least two of these ruffians. Unfortunately three of the men carried heavy flintlock pistols, deadly at close range.

"You are making a grave mistake, Colonel Thiebaldt. This action will cost you dearly in the future." Gen. Waverly ignored the quick glance from Dr. Frank.

"If we cannot persuade the delegation to see the future as we have proposed it, I have none." Thiebaldt nodded toward the door. "Remove them!"

"It's simple and complex at the same time, Colonel," Ruth said. "How much do you know about this project?"

"Damned little. The general said it was highly specialized and that my mission was to provide outside security. Where is General Waverly?"

Dr. Ruth Hampstead sighed, "The project…"

"We'll get to the project in a moment," Thiebaldt snapped. "Where is General Waverly?"

"We believe General Waverly, Dr. Frank, and Dr. Mason have all been transported into the past."

"Into the past? Do you think I'm an idiot?" His eyes glittering, Lt. Col. Thiebaldt studied the three visitors. "And who are these people and where did they come from?"

"The project," Ruth said, her voice hard, "was an attempt to peek into the past, to eavesdrop on a small dinner party."

Thiebaldt continued to stare at the visitors. "How?"

Ruth took a deep breath. "Utilizing massive amounts of power in an enclosed electromagnetic array which…"

"When and where?" he asked.

"Right here in Philadelphia," Annie said. "In 1787."

The two soldiers behind Thiebaldt eyed each other in disbelief.

"That's why you people received so much R&D funds." Theibaldt's eyebrows rose slightly but the eyes continued to glitter. "So you succeeded and then somebody goofed," he said, "…and there was a transfer."

"We're going to take our guests over to my house," Annie said. "While Dr. Hampstead fixes the electronics so we can reverse the process."

"Not so fast," Thiebaldt said. "My grasp of history is pretty good. If I'm not mistaken, you have delivered George Washington, Benjamin Franklin, and James Madison to the 21st century."

"Delivered isn't the term I would use," Annie said.

"But that's the case." Theibaldt's mouth looked so tight it seemed a miracle to see him speak. "Exactly when in 1787?"

"May 13th," Franklin said. "Does that possess any significance for you?"

Thiebaldt fixed his gaze on Washington. "If memory serves,

that's early on in the Constitutional Convention."

"What an intriguing title," Franklin said with smile. "At the time of our, ah, departure, we were about to amend the Articles of Confederation."

"Colonel," Annie said quickly. "Please don't say anything further, we don't want to change history."

Theibaldt's eyes cut at her. "Of course not, Miss Malone. Who knows what could happen. As head of project security I'm going to arrange secure accommodations for our 'guests.' You all stay right here until I return. Sergeant," he said over his shoulder, "...nobody goes through that door without my permission, you got that?"

"Yes, Sir!" The sergeant snapped to attention.

"I shouldn't be gone long. In the meantime, the rest of you just take it easy. And I want to find all of you here when I return."

Thiebaldt and the corporal exited.

Annie stared at the sergeant. "Strange situation, isn't it, Jerry?"

The sergeant swallowed and frowned. "Sure is, Annie. I never thought I'd be guarding my own girlfriend."

"Girlfriend?" Ruth said, looking from Annie to the sergeant and back. "I knew you had a boyfriend, but I didn't know he was in the military."

"Subject never came up," Annie said. "Until now it didn't seem important."

"You and this young man," Franklin pointed at Jerry, "...have an intimate connection?"

"Had," Annie said. "Much depends on him if it's to continue."

"Annie," Jerry said. "There's not a problem here. I'm only following orders."

"Jerry, I know you want to be an army officer. But you are also sworn to uphold the Constitution of the United States, right?"

"Yeah, but–"

"What you are doing is illegal. Your job is provide security from outside this building, not the other way around. What right does Thiebaldt have to confine us?"

"He's worried about General Waverly."

"No. He's figuring out how to take advantage of this situation. Is this any way to greet honored guests from the past?"

Jerry nodded toward the visitors. "They're really who the colonel said they were?"

"Yes." Annie glanced at the visitors. "So why can't we leave?"

"I'm sure it has to do with their security," Jerry said, as a deep flush spread upwards from his neck. "I've got one more year of college before I'm commissioned. I'm going to follow orders."

"Even if it means making a prisoner out of the woman you claim to love?" Annie snapped.

"If that's what it takes!" he snapped back.

Nick waved his hand. "Hey, Jerry–"

"That's 'Sergeant Burdock' to you!" Jerry grated.

"Oh. Excuse me, Sergeant Burdock. Do you have a problem with us working on our equipment?" Nick jabbed a thumb toward his console.

"Go ahead, but if your spare parts aren't in house, you can forget it until the Colonel comes back."

"Thanks." Nick sat down and began mumbling to Ruth.

"Sergeant Burdock," Annie said with scorn. "You may consider our relationship finished."

Dr. Mason tugged on the door. "It's locked. What are we going to do now?"

General Waverly moved about the storeroom, testing the few windows, pulling on the larger doors at the other end of the room. "Do you know where we are, Mrs. Conner?"

"I believe we are in Hiram Winford's warehouse. He deals in dry goods when he isn't playing soldier." She nodded to Gen. Waverly. "No disrespect intended, sir."

"None taken, ma'am."

"He served honorably in the war, and his poor wife kept the business going. Now that the war is over, Mrs. Winford is still running things, and Hiram just gads about with those ruffians who locked us in here."

"Is it possible the constable knows of this?" Dr. Frank asked.

"Heavens, no! He'd have us out in a trice and those men would be in stocks."

"We need to get out of here," Gen. Waverly said. "But first we have to find different clothes." He looked down at his uniform. "We stick out like a sore thumb here."

"This is a dry goods warehouse," Dr. Mason said. "Perhaps there might be clothing in some of these boxes?"

"Clothing, sir?" Mrs. Conner said. "This isn't a tailor's shop. The best to be found here would be bolts of cloth."

"What's up there?" Gen. Waverly asked, pointing to where a wall-mounted ladder stopped at a square panel in the flat ceiling.

"General," Mrs. Conner said with some testiness. "I have never before entered this building. I possess no knowledge of its contents or construction."

"Sorry, Mrs. Conner. I always ask you first because you're our resident expert." General Waverly climbed the ladder and pushed the panel upward. "Well, it's not locked." He disappeared through the opening.

Dr. Mason peered at Mrs. Conner. "How well do you know this Colonel Thiebaldt?"

"The first time I ever laid eyes on him was when he pushed through Dr. Franklin's door today."

"If we can get away from these people," Dr. Frank waved his hand at the storeroom, "is there anyone who might help us?"

"Young Mr. Hamilton would. He places great devotion and allegiance on General Washington."

"Alexander Hamilton?" Dr. Frank said.

"He is the only Mr. Hamilton I am aware of."

"Excuse me," General Waverly peered down from the trap door. "Are there bolts of cloth, heavy cloth, down there?"

Mrs. Conner glanced about with a practiced eye. "Yes, General, here are bolts of sail cloth."

"Excellent! Gentlemen, please hand me up two bolts and then all of you come up here as quickly as you can."

Dr. Mason grabbed a bolt. "My word! This is much heavier than I thought it would be. Give me a hand here, Frank."

The two men handed the bolt up to where General Waverly could reach it. The general grasped it with one hand and easily lifted it into the attic. The academics shared an expression of surprise before grabbing the second bolt.

"Mrs. Conner," Dr. Frank indicated the ladder.

"If you please, gentlemen," she said with a slight blush, brushing at her long dress, "I'll follow you."

"Oh, of course." Dr. Frank hurried to the ladder, his face already flushed from his labors.

In moments they all peered about in the gloomy attic.

"Over here," Waverly said. He slid a window up and edged open the heavy shutters. Pale light gleamed through the opening and the general peered out.

"Here's my plan." he motioned them forward, pointed down. "There's another building butted up against this one. Its roof is only ten or twelve feet below us. We can make a rope out of the sail cloth and slide down."

"Then what?" Dr. Mason said. "Yell for help and be caught by those zealots?"

Waverly fixed him with a level stare. "If you'll allow me to finish? That's why I asked for two bolts. We reconnoiter and get to the ground at the safest place."

"Excellent idea, General," Dr. Frank said. "Then we can make our way to Mr. Hamilton's and ask his help."

Waverly scratched his jaw. "I thought you wanted to make as few waves as possible here. Do we really need to involve Mr. Hamilton?"

"Point taken, sir." Dr. Frank's gaze moved over them. "However, these zealots, as Dr. Mason appropriately described them, are armed and obviously dangerous. We are at a definite disadvantage."

"Yes and no," Waverly said. "They had three pistols. Horse pistols to be exact. They can be deadly at close range, but at anything over 20 feet they are wildly inaccurate, even in the hands of a marksman. I have great doubts that any of our friends could be classified as marksmen."

"You're betting our lives on that," Dr. Mason snapped. "I think we should stay right here and hope that Nick Gordon remedies this situation."

"I'd like to point out," Dr. Frank said, "that we are not in the target area of the probe. So even if Nick and Annie fix the apparatus, they cannot find us here. Also, I'd like to back up General Waverly's observation about the accuracy of horse pistols. This is before the development of rifled barrels."

Dr. Mason frowned. "That's true. Not to mention that it's already dark and getting darker. Very well, I vote we carry out General Waverly's plan."

General Waverly smiled. "Mrs. Conner, do you know the way back to Dr. Franklin's house from here?"

"Of course I do. But you were right when you said your clothing would excite comment on the street, even in lantern light. And why do you not wish to see Mr. Hamilton?"

General Waverly nodded toward Dr. Frank. "Perhaps our resident historian would care to answer that one?" He started tying knots every two feet in the sailcloth.

"We wish to avoid changing history, Mrs. Conner," Dr. Frank said. "But, unfortunately, I'm afraid we already have."

"And I fear we must change it even further," Dr. Mason said, peering out the window. "They've left a sentry."

Nick and Ruth muttered to one another as they worked. Annie glared at Jerry whenever her gaze crossed his, but mostly she ignored him. The three visitors sat in the folding chairs most recently used by their counterparts misplaced in time.

Washington and Madison conferred in whispers as Franklin listened. Washington's head lifted, "Miss Malone, would you attend us, please?"

Annie took a chair next to them. "Yes, General?"

"Mr. Madison and I are well acquainted with Colonel Theibaldt's ancestor."

"I gathered that from what we heard before the accident," she said.

Madison inched closer. "General Washington and I feel that your Colonel Thiebaldt is not to be trusted with our persons."

"Gentlemen, I couldn't agree more," Annie said. "But we seem to be in custody."

Washington's smile looked deadly. "He is but one man, easily subdued."

"Uh, I know Jerry. He's pretty strong and knows his way around in the martial arts. Don't let him know you're going to take him out."

Washington cracked his knuckles. "Take him out, indeed. Very well, we shall not be sporting. You gain his attention and leave the rest to me."

"Wait a few minutes, if we all move now he'll know something is up. I'll nod to you and one minute later I'll distract him."

Washington nodded. Franklin grinned widely. "This has turned out to be such an interesting evening!"

"You ain't seen nothin' yet," Annie said with a grin as she got to her feet. She walked over to the console, feeling distressed when she saw components lying around the open cavity.

As if reading her mind, Nick said, "This looks worse than it really is. We've figured out the problem, and we think we can be back to where things went wiggy in about five hours. Right, Ruth?"

"Concur," Ruth said without looking away from her work.

"Okay, here's the deal," Annie said. She told them about

Washington's plan.

"He's going to jump Jerry?" Nick asked.

"Why don't you just shout it all over the city?" Annie hissed.

"Sorry." Nick lowered his voice. "Does Washington know about karate and all that?"

"Let's find out," Annie said with more aplomb than she felt. She looked into the general's eyes and nodded. "Okay, we're counting down a minute here," she whispered. "Don't look at Jerry, whatever you do."

"Y'know," Ruth whispered. "Despite the fact that you're a liberal arts major and don't know beans about journeyman physics, I like you. But if you didn't want us to know about your antics, why did you bring it up?"

"I didn't want to surprise either of you," Annie said in a hurt tone.

"Your minute is up in six seconds," Nick said.

Annie straightened up and shouted, "To hell with you, Jerry!"

Sergeant Jerry Burdock, startled and defensive, automatically slid into a karate stance facing her. Washington caught him totally unawares; closing the distance between them in two steps he hit Jerry in the jaw with a massive fist.

Jerry bounced off the wall and landed in a heap at Washington's feet. The General shook his right hand loosely and grimaced. "I haven't done that in years. Quite forgot how much it could hurt."

"Ruth, do you need Nick to get that done?" Annie asked.

"Not really. Might take me an extra half hour of reaching for things he could hand me, but that's it."

"Great. Nick, where's your car?"

"Out back. I don't try to park on the street."

"Superb. Gentlemen," Annie smiled at the visitors, "we're going for a ride you won't believe. I have to ask all of you to do exactly as I say, when I say it. I will tell you when you can ask more questions. Okay, Dr. Franklin?"

"What does 'okay' mean?" Franklin asked.

"Succinctly, it means; do you agree to that?"

"I wish to learn the etymology of the term, but, yes!"

"Great. We're going to go out and get into a conveyance we call an automobile, or car."

Franklin opened his mouth, but Annie pressed on. "Then we're going to go somewhere I won't mention now, because if

Ruth doesn't know, she can't tell Colonel Thiebaldt."

Ruth glanced up, grinning. "Concur."

Annie hurried to the door, opened it a crack and peeked out. "Colonel Thiebaldt has a lot of confidence in Jerry, there are no guards outside. Nick, take up the rear. Everyone follow me."

She slipped out the door.

George Washington followed on her heels. James Madison gestured to Benjamin Franklin to precede him, and Franklin limped after the general.

Nick looked at Ruth. "We'll be back in six hours. Have the thing ready to go."

"What if I crank it up and our people aren't there?"

"We'll worry about it then."

"Have a wonderful time," Ruth said with a nasty grin.

"General Waverly is correct," Dr. Frank said from his station at the window. "The sentry takes exactly nine minutes to make one round."

Dr. Mason wiped sweat from his brow. "Can you see the general?"

"No. And it seems our sentry can't, either."

"What can the man be waiting for?" Mrs. Conner said peevishly.

"He's not," Dr. Frank said with barely suppressed animation. "He just stepped up to the fellow and knocked him senseless. Come along, he's waving us down."

"I must admit, I am surprised," Dr. Frank said as the four of them moved along the quiet street behind the warehouse.

"At what? General Waverly asked.

"Nobody else seems to have seen us."

"No surprise," Mrs. Conner said. "Most of the citizens of Philadelphia have their dinner at this hour."

"Dinner," Dr. Mason said. "I had planned to dine after watching this experiment fail once again."

"Nick has an exceptional mind," Dr. Frank said. "Why do you hold so little regard for him?"

"I thought him a fool." Mason sounded defeated. "He went where I thought there was no possible chance of success. Think about it - time travel?"

"My word," Mrs. Conner said. "There's a landau!"

She hurried out into the middle of the street and hailed a horse-drawn carriage. "Gentlemen, please stay with me."

They climbed into the coach behind her. She rapped on the partition between them and the driver. "Mr. Hamilton's house, if you please."

The driver snapped his whip in the air and they set off at a brisk pace down the cobbled street.

General Waverly nudged Dr. Frank. "Tell me about Hamilton,"

"Well," he hesitated and darted a look at Mrs. Conner who sat back in total shadow.

"Gentlemen, I work for a very peculiar man and I keep his confidences. Say what you will, I assure you it will go no further."

She plucked at her skirt and her face caught passing light as she peered out the window.

"Very well," Dr. Frank said. "Alexander Hamilton is a brilliant man, especially in the fields of economics and government. From what I have read, he is arrogant to a fault, probably stemming from his illegitimate birth in the West Indies."

"Over-compensation?" General Waverly asked.

"That would be my guess, but I'm a historian, not a psychologist. He's completely loyal to General Washington, and has absolutely no royalist leanings."

"Therefore he won't be part of this Cincinnati business?" Dr. Mason asked.

"Exactly," Dr. Frank said. "He's probably quite antagonistic toward them."

"But he's a veteran?" General Waverly pressed.

"Oh, yes. Incredibly brave, served with distinction during the War for Independence," Dr. Frank said. "In fact he was Washington's adjutant."

"I'll back up that assessment," Mrs. Conner said. "Despite the unfortunate circumstances of his birth, Mr. Hamilton is held in high regard in Philadelphia even though he actually resides in New York. Dr. Franklin and General Washington both call on him for all manner of problems."

"Then you believe he will aid us?" General Waverly said to Mrs. Conner.

"Without a doubt. He knows me and what I stand for," she said in a crisp tone. "It's a good thing you gentlemen have me along, you'd play hob obtaining help else."

"Good lady," Waverly said with a slow smile. "Your presence does me more good than would a regiment of regulars."

Mrs. Conner sniffed. "I dare say, General Waverly, but I suspect you might be a bit of a rogue."

"I plead guilty and throw myself on the mercy of the court!"

"Good God, General!" Dr. Mason snapped. "This is no time to lose yourself in a flirt."

Dr. Frank coughed and peered intently out the window.

"For the record," General Waverly said evenly. "I think you could profit from a flirt or two, yourself, Dr. Mason. And, in the future, or here in the past, I'll take it poorly if you have the effrontery to again comment on my personal behavior."

"Oh! I assure you, sir, I meant no umbrage. Yes, quite sorry, yes."

Dr. Frank coughed again and massaged his jaw.

The coach stopped. "Colonel Hamilton's house, Ma'am," the driver called out.

Mrs. Conner gave the coachman a coin. "Will that do, sir?"

He peered at the coin and tentatively bit it. "Good enough, ma'am, thank ye."

"What kind of coin was that, Mrs. Conner?" Dr. Frank asked.

"One of the Connecticut dollars, I believe. Why?"

"It just struck me that there's a numismatic treasure trove all around me…"

"Doctor," General Waverly said with a growl, "We don't have the time for hobbies right now." He pointed toward the house.

Dr. Frank obediently moved forward, glancing back at the military man. "Consider the plethora of antique firearms within a mile of us, all in pristine condition."

Waverly faltered for a moment but continued walking. "Satan, get thee behind me." he said with grin.

"What's a numismatic?" Mrs. Conner asked as they reached the door.

Before anyone could answer, or knock, the door swung open. The well-lit entry revealed a short, stout man with three chins, jowls, and a wig that appeared to have been fashioned from uncombed white straw.

"An' what kin I do fer yez?" he said in a surly tone.

Mrs. Conner squared her shoulders. "You may inform Mr. Hamilton that Mrs. Conner, Dr. Franklin's housekeeper, and three well-traveled gentlemen, would appreciate a moment of his time anon if it might be convenient."

The man scowled. "Mr. Hamilton's a very busy man, he is, and the hour be late. What would be the nature of yer business, now?"

Color stood out high on Mrs. Conner's face and she took a deep breath.

"Enoch!" a voice said from within. "Show those people in immediately!"

"Yes, sir, Mr. Hamilton," Enoch said with a grudging air. He stepped aside and bobbed in pretense of a bow as Mrs. Conner sailed past him like a ship of the line overhauling a scow.

As General Waverly passed, Enoch glared up at him, his jaw

working. Waverly stared back impassively and moved on.

Dr. Frank stared at Alexander Hamilton in unabashed awe. He knew all about this man; that he was out of favor with the rest of New York's delegation; that he would absent the convention midway but return before it finished; that his pride would be the cause of his ultimate downfall and death at the hands of Aaron Burr. He knew he beheld the genius who would give the United States the working economy needed to make it a viable nation.

"Mrs. Conner, this is a most unexpected visit," Hamilton said, keeping his violet eyes on her.

"For all of us, sir," she said and curtsied. "I humbly beg your pardon, but I knew no where else to turn in a time of need."

"Dr. Franklin has need of my services?"

"In a matter of speaking…"

General Waverly's casual cough broke through her nervousness.

"I'm forgetting my manners. Allow me to present General Waverly, Dr. Frank, and Dr. Mason, who have all traveled a great distance to be here this evening."

Hamilton nodded at each man in turn. "You gentlemen are from a foreign country, no doubt, as I do not recognize your style of clothing."

General Waverly opened his mouth, but Dr. Frank seized the initiative.

"Good sir, let me begin by saying how much I admire you and your ideas."

A tinge of rose softened Hamilton's alabaster cheeks, and the nostrils of his fine, porcelain-like nose testified to his sharp intake of breath. "Thank you, Dr. Frank, such effusive appreciation is quite rare these days, not even the citizens of my home state hold me as highly as you seem to. And where did you say you hailed from?"

"Well, in a manner of speaking, you and we are countrymen. However, we are not contemporaries." Dr. Frank glanced at his fellow travelers, who both nodded, before continuing, "You are familiar with Dr. Franklin's experiments?"

"With some. The good doctor possesses a voracious curiosity whose limits astound and elude me. Is there a particular experiment to which you refer?"

"Ah, no. Not really. But the subject sets the stage for what I must tell you next."

Hamilton's eyebrows rose slightly.

"My two companions and I are from the United States of America."

"Indeed? Which state do you call home, and are you fellow delegates to the assembly?"

"We are not delegates, alas. And I fear you would not recognize the names of our home states. We are from the future."

"As Enoch said, I am a very busy man." Color heightened in his cheeks. "I have no time to spare for riddles, conundrums, or mad men."

"Mr. Hamilton," Mrs. Conner said quickly. "Please hear him out, I vouch for his words."

"Only because I know you are a level-headed woman of intelligence, and in the service of a dear friend, will I listen further. You have five minutes, Dr. Frank."

Dr. Frank took three minutes to encapsulate the situation.

"When are you from?" Hamilton asked, visibly shaken.

"2019 A.D." Dr. Frank repeated.

"And Dr. Franklin, General Washington, and Mr. Madison are stranded in that year at this moment?"

"Just as we are in this year of 1787," Dr. Frank said with an emphatic nod.

"Pray, give me a moment." Hamilton turned and left the room.

"Has he gone for a weapon?" Dr. Mason asked.

"You will suffer no harm at Mr. Hamilton's hand," Mrs. Conner snapped. "Give the man time to grasp this impossibility."

Hamilton walked back into the room. "What is it you wish of me?"

"Transportation and a body guard," Mrs. Conner said.

General Waverly held up his hand. "I'd like to amend that, Mr. Hamilton; transportation and hand weapons. I would ask for nothing more."

Hamilton nodded but didn't move. "Tell me, is the convention successful? Will we come to agreement on the Articles of Confederation?"

Dr. Frank shook his head. "I cannot tell you more than this; the Articles of Confederation are as dead as General Braddock."

"I feared as much," Hamilton said, his face paling even more. "Come along, I think the three of you need less excitable clothes before I send you away."

Philadelphia - 2019

General Washington and James Madison hurried into the parking lot behind Nick. Dr. Franklin, limping with gout, moved even slower as he beheld the vehicles in the parking lot, the electric wires overhead, and the light-filled cityscape surrounding them.

"What manner engines are these?" he asked Annie, waving his walking stick.

"Follow your friends!" she snapped. "This is no time for a question and answer period."

Franklin chuckled. "Your professed awe has quickly transformed into brusque familiarity, Miss Malone."

"Necessity requires it, sir. I still find you a fascinating person."

"How far does your interest extend?" he asked as he hobbled along.

"Dr. Franklin! Are you coming on to me?"

"I do not recognize the expression, Miss Malone."

"Are you attempting to seduce me?"

"Well, frankly, yes." He grinned at her.

"While I find you a fascinating man, brilliant scientist, and extraordinary statesman, I have absolutely no interest in physical congress with you."

"You are very erudite for a woman," Franklin said in a subdued tone.

"And Abrigale Adams isn't?" Annie shot back.

"Not to my knowledge," Franklin said in surprise.

You will never meet her again, Annie thought.

She knew Franklin had three years left, most of which would be spent in Philadelphia. Abrigale Adams wouldn't leave Braintree, Massachusetts until 1797, when she accompanied her husband to the new capital city as First Lady.

"When next I am in her presence I will endeavor to converse with her," Franklin said. "The deity alone knows when that will be." He cast Annie a sly glance that she ignored.

Nick's 1988 Chevy van probably didn't have three years left. Rust cancered the body in many places, the windshield bore a crack from top to bottom on the far right side, and once he got the engine started, the valves clattered like castanets for the better part of a minute.

Annie checked the visitors. Washington's jaw line stood out, easily dominating the neck pouches that men of his age develop. The whites of Madison's eyes proved easily discernable and he gripped the armrest with both hands. Franklin sat between them avidly watching the ignition procedure. "What manner of magic propels this vehicle?"

"It's called an internal combustion engine," Nick explained as he backed out of his parking place.

Annie searched about for the military security she feared must be close.

"The engine is made out of iron and steel and runs on a petroleum distillate called gasoline," Nick continued as he slowly drove through the parking lot. "This is an old van. Most of the new ones run on electricity or natural gas."

"Steel is an element? You steer easily with the wheel you hold, fascinating." Franklin glanced out at the ranks of parked cars and trucks. The parking lot never seemed to empty. "There are so many, what did you call it, vans?"

They neared the exit to the street. Half a block ahead, cruising slowly toward them through the parking lot, came the unmistakable shape of a Humvee.

"Nick!" Annie blurted.

"I see them. Don't worry, they don't know who we are." He turned into the exit, glanced left and then accelerated into the street. "Besides, we're outta here."

Annie glanced back at their passengers. All three stared out the windows. Madison caught Annie's gaze. "Isn't this a rather precipitous rate of speed?"

Annie glanced at the speedometer, Nick was doing 45 in a 30MPH zone. "Yes," she said loudly in Nick's ear, "...we are going at a precipitous rate. In fact we're speeding at a time when we can't afford to get stopped!"

Nick scowled at her. "Okay, I get the message!"

The van slowed. Other vehicles whizzed past them as if they were stationary.

"This is still quite fast," Madison said.

"We live in a much faster world than yours, Mr. Madison," Annie said. "This van could, if the road would allow, probably carry you eighty miles in an hour."

"In an hour!" Franklin exclaimed. "But wait, first tell me

about the road, it seems uncommon smooth and handsomely constructed."

"Well put, Doctor. It is made with asphalt, yet another by-product of petroleum."

"The substance that powers this van?"

"Very different, but related."

"Where do you obtain this petroleum?" Washington asked.

"Out of the ground," Annie replied. "It's called 'oil' and it stinks."

"I know the stuff!" Franklin exclaimed with an air of excitement. "It's quite gravid and dark, tastes wretched."

"It dominated the 20th Century." Annie glanced behind them, saw red flashing lights. "Nick?"

"Yeah, I see them. Where can we go?"

"Left at the light and then step on it."

Nick went through a red light and stomped on the gas. The van lurched and tore down the street, rapidly catching up with traffic.

"All this illumination," Franklin muttered, "even the streets shine bright as day."

"There's an alley there on the right, take it!" Annie ordered.

"Jeeze!" Nick hit the brake and the van rocked violently to the left as he made the turn. "Give me a bit of warning next time, okay?"

"You turned before they got to the intersection." she said, looking out the back window. "Go right at the street and then make the first left you come to. Good driving, by the way."

All three visitors clutched armrests. Madison's eyes resembled saucers, Washington appeared to be grinding his teeth, and Franklin actually panted through his partially opened mouth, eyes wide and flicking eagerly across the rapidly passing scenery.

"Gentlemen," Annie said, trying to sound calm. "We need to elude the military police. We'll soon be in a safe place."

"We certainly are not in one now!" Washington snapped.

"Verily," Franklin said. "Your laws are enforced by the military?"

The van swerved to the left.

"Now which way?"

"Take the second right, down three blocks and then left again. No, doctor, but our project had military security because the government provided a large part of our funding."

Nick's mouth pressed into a flat line and his eyes narrowed as he cut off an instantly honking limo in order to make the next turn. "You know where we're going or are we just in evasion mode?"

"We're going to my place."

"Doesn't the sergeant know where you live?"

"We're not staying long."

"Whatever you say."

All three visitors emitted sighs of relief when Nick shut off the van in Annie's driveway.

"Is this the haven you mentioned earlier?" Washington asked.

"No, we're going to change vehicles here, they know Nick's van, but they don't know my Volvo."

"Won't that be a little cramped?" Nick said, stretching until his back cracked.

"It's a sedan. The back seat is huge."

"I won't ask, 'huge enough for what?'"

Annie scowled at him. "Everybody inside, we'll get food and water." She led the way.

As soon as she snapped on the lights, she wished she had left everyone in the van. She hadn't cleaned house for at least six weeks. The project had absorbed all of her time.

Dr. Franklin limped into the living room and dropped his bulk on the sofa. "You mentioned a potion that cures gout?"

"Oh, right." She hurried into the bathroom, returned in moments. "Here, take two, I'll get you some water." She handed Franklin the plastic bottle.

Franklin carefully read the bottle label, and then tugged on the cap. Annie returned with a glass of water. "Here you are, Dr. Franklin."

"The cork seems to be stuck in this bottle."

"Oh, it's not a cork. Let me show you." She explained the mechanics of the pill bottle, and watched him open it twice.

"This material, what is it?"

"Plastic," Nick said from where he stood by the window. "Yet another petroleum product. Eighty percent of consumer products in the world are made of plastic."

Franklin showed the bottle to his fellow time travelers. "How do the artisans work this material?" Hamilton asked.

Nick quickly explained injection mold machines. "I used to run one when I was an undergraduate. I made about a thousand spoons an hour with mine."

"What do they do with so many spoons?" Washington asked, his forehead furrowing at the numbers.

"People use them once and then they throw them away,"

"Throw them away?" Franklin exclaimed. "Why such extravagance?"

Nick shrugged. "They're cheap to make, hard to clean, and there's always more where the last one came from."

All three visitors fell silent, staring at the young man.

"Nick," Annie yelled from the kitchen. "How about some help?"

He jumped to his feet and hurried into her. "I don't think they approve of what we've done with the country," he whispered.

"Neither do I. There's some paper plates up there, I can't reach them."

He snagged the plastic bag and pulled it down. "Where are we going from here?"

"To Dr. Frank's house. I'm pretty sure he's not home. Let's get out of here."

"You all look like prosperous merchants," Mrs. Conner said. "Especially you, General Waverly."

"Just as long as nobody thinks I'm a slave."

Hamilton snorted. "You carry yourself like a potentate. No one would think you a slave."

Waverly flashed a wide smile. "I'll take that as a compliment, Mr. Hamilton. Thank you."

Hamilton's features softened. "Merely stating the obvious, my good general."

Dr. Frank fixedly regarded his unfamiliar clothing. "I never thought I'd find myself blending in by wearing silk pantaloons."

"Have the splinter members of the Society of the Cincinnati approached you, Mr. Hamilton?" Dr. Mason asked.

"In stupefying repetition." Hamilton produced a lace handkerchief and touched it to his nose. "They would have us believe them gentlemen rather than the opportunistic rabble they truly are."

"You don't think the United States needs a house of lords?" Waverly asked.

"No." Hamilton fixed his gaze on a pair of crossed swords flanked by a battle flag from the war, all tastefully displayed on an otherwise blank wall. "The British House of Lords represents only wealth, privilege, and stagnation. Not the forward thinking intelligence this country needs to survive."

"Well said, sir." Dr. Mason bowed awkwardly from the waist and swept the lavender, lace-edged tricorner off his head so fast that he dropped it on the carpeted floor.

"You seem to take your current situation as a farce, sir," Hamilton snapped. "If that be the case, I refuse to use my name and station to aid you further."

Mason grabbed the hat and snapped upright, his face pale. "I meant no such thing. I merely sought to release my tension with a trifling of levity. If you felt insult, I humbly apologize."

Hamilton awarded him a ghost of a smile. "You are nimble on your mental feet, Dr. Mason. You would go far here."

"As General Waverly said, you are very complimentary." Dr. Mason hesitated, then added, "I will be honest, sir. This situation frightens me more than anything I ever before encountered."

Hamilton nodded sharply and, looking away, said, "I understand."

"We are ready, Mr. Hamilton," Mrs. Conner said. "By the way, where are your lovely wife and fine sons?"

"They visit family in Boston, more the pity. I feel certain this event would color their conversation for years."

"The less conversation about us, the better," Dr. Frank said.

"I have been ruminating on the very fact of your presence," Hamilton said. "It is obvious to me that the United States will not only endure, but prosper. That whatever accommodation we agree to at the State House will carry this infant country through at least two centuries."

The three visitors regarded him silently. Dr. Frank's eyes seemed hooded. Dr. Mason wiped his sweaty brow and rolled his eyes from one fellow traveler to the other.

"We cannot engage in a conversation on that subject, Mr. Hamilton," General Waverly said, "I'm sure you can appreciate that."

When Hamilton smiled, he appeared fox-like. "Your uniform reticence quite supports my contention. My carriage is ready, shall we journey to Dr. Franklin's house?"

"You're going with us?" General Waverly asked.

"Were we able to exchange circumstances, wouldn't you?"

"What had you planned to do today, sir?" Dr. Frank asked.

"Relax so that I may be fresh for the battle facing me on the morrow. But now I think perhaps the tonic of your unique situation will serve me better."

"Perhaps," Dr. Mason said, "You are the one taking this as a farce."

"Not at all. I know the secrets of the ages stand mute before me and I would be worse than a fool to not discover all that I might." He offered Mrs. Conner his arm. "Please follow us, gentlemen."

Annie followed Nick in his van and waited while he parked in a twenty-four lot near downtown. They decided the risk of apprehension was worth hiding the vehicle away from her house. In moments he jumped into the front seat of the Volvo.

"I have noticed a general similarity of your locomotive machines," Dr. Franklin said from the back seat. But yet they all seem to differ in minute ways. Why is that?"

Annie drove while Nick tried to explain Detroit marketing plans.

"This must be a very rich country," Washington murmured. "To support the rate of manufacture you describe, the average citizen must be wealthy beyond belief."

Nick groaned. "No, General Washington, not quite. They also invented a thing called 'credit'."

Annie tuned them out as she drove. Her passengers didn't notice as she circled a ring of blocks before making a left and repeating her action on a smaller ring. Jerry Burdock had once explained military surveillance tactics to her. Now she had reason to test his knowledge.

She made a right turn just before they would have passed Dr. Frank's house and almost gasped as they passed a late model sedan with two men in the front seat, parked in front of a fire hydrant. The driver stared fixedly in the direction of Dr. Frank's house but the other snapped his head around and held her gaze for a full three seconds.

Annie forced herself to feign indifference and turn her attention back to her driving. She watched the rear-view mirror but the sedan didn't move.

"We can't go to Dr. Frank's house," she said tersely.

"Why not?" Nick asked, breaking off his explanation of credit ratings.

"They're watching it."

"You sure? How could they-"

"Dammit, Nick! I just drove by two goons who had their eyes glued on his front door. We're not going there."

"Okay. Whatever. Don't blow a synapse."

"There are agents already watching our destination?" Washington asked.

"'Fraid so," Annie said.

"How could they be summoned so quickly?" Franklin queried.

Annie tuned out Nick's overview of modern communications, cell phones, electronic snoopers, bugs, taps, and all their kin. Where could she take them? If they kept moving their chances of apprehension grew.

Thiebaldt had pulled in more than military intelligence on this, she decided. "Oh, wow!" she blurted, startling all four men. "Of course!"

"What?" Nick snapped.

"The Phi Alpha Theta party," she said, smiling sweetly while making a left turn.

"We're going to a frat party?" Nick's tone dripped with sarcasm. "Don't we need togas for that?"

"Phi Alpha Theta is the history honor society. The chapter is having a costume party tonight. I got an invitation but blew it off because of the project."

"You're sure it's tonight?"

"Graduate students in history don't forget dates."

The closest parking place was a block from the party. As Franklin eased his bulk out of the Volvo, he kicked an empty Dr. Pepper bottle.

"Mr. Madison, would you be so good as to retrieve that for me?"

Madison gently picked it up and handed it to Franklin. Both men regarded it as if it were made from gold. "Has someone misplaced a treasure?" Franklin asked.

"It's just a used plastic bottle, trash," Nick said.

Franklin ran his fingers over every millimeter of the bottle before dropping it. "Trash," he murmured.

A Boeing 787 thundered overhead and all three travelers fastened their attention on the blinking lights soaring through the night.

"Aircraft," Nick said before any of them could find their tongue. "Flying machines that carry people from one city to another. I'll explain later."

Washington grabbed Franklin before the older man could do more than sag to his knees. "A hand here!" he snapped.

Nick grabbed the man's other arm and helped Washington straighten the old scientist to his feet. Franklin peered owlishly at him.

"You, you said, 'a flying machine that carries people'?"

"Yes, sir. I'm sorry I startled you like that. People have been flying for just over a century. We've even gone to the m-"

"Nick!" Annie snapped. "Enough!"

"Quite," Franklin said. "As it is, I think I need a physic."

"Where we're going you'll be able to get anything liquid, except maybe water." Annie smiled at Franklin and the color came back into his face.

"There are rules for this party," she said. Most of the people will be in costume, portraying historical figures. You three gentlemen are very likely to meet copies of yourselves. The first rule is to stay in character - if you are caught saying something the historical personage wouldn't have said, or couldn't know, you get a mark on your forehead.

"Second, if you catch another person remarking out of character, you get to give them one of your marks. Third, the object of the party is to have fun and see how good a grasp you have of history."

Annie slowed and looked up at Washington. "General, please don't take offense at anything anyone says tonight. You're probably going to get a lot of guff because you were, are, a slave owner."

"Guff?"

"Lampoons, digs, snide comments."

"Slavery is something I grew up with, it's as ingrained in Virginia as religion and horse racing. I know slavery is the prime abomination of the three, but I doubt any of them will end in my day."

"Just wanted to give you heads up on that, you too, Mr. Madison." Annie said, pursing her lips. "Okay, let's go party."

As Alexander Hamilton's coach jiggled them over the cobbled streets, all four men kept careful watch of those they passed.

"I want you to understand, gentlemen," Hamilton said. "There are many in the Society of the Cincinnati who are honorable and dedicated. Unfortunately, Colonel Thiebaldt, who is only dedicated to furthering his own career and fortune, has gathered a group of like-minded confederates who back his insane notions."

"Why hasn't something been done about this madman?" Dr. Mason asked.

"I suppose," Hamilton said, "it would depend on one's viewpoint whether Thiebaldt should be considered a madman or a visionary. These are strange times, Dr. Mason."

"But he kidnapped us!" Dr. Mason said.

"And he and his cronies invaded Dr. Franklin's home to do it," Hamilton added. "This is indeed enough to have him arrested and jailed. But you gentlemen would have to press charges against him, and I'm not sure you wish to have more notice brought to bear on your presence."

"My God, no," Dr. Frank blurted.

"Quite so. Therefore we must deal with him and his associates."

"I've never fired one of these before," General Waverly said, twisting the flintlock pistol so that the ambient light played across the barrel, pan, and hammer. "But I've fired many hand weapons in my life, and I'm sure this one will suffice nicely."

"Would that I could see the weapons with which you are intimate," Hamilton said.

A small panel in the front of the coach slid open. "We're approaching Dr. Franklin's house, Mr. Hamilton," the coachman said in a low voice.

"Thank you Bandry. Nothing has changed, just follow my instructions."

"Yes, sir." The panel slid shut.

"Why must the three of you remain at Dr. Franklin's house where you risk rediscovery? My home is much safer, I assure you."

"The machine that malfunctioned is limited as to, ah, target site." Dr. Mason cleared his throat. "We must be where we were delivered in order to be returned to our own time. For all we know, our people could be scanning Dr. Franklin's dining room as we speak."

"Scanning? I do not know that term."

"Searching with a machine," General Waverly said."

"There's Franklin's house," Dr. Frank said with wariness in his voice.

"Bandry will pass the house and then go around the block on which it sits, Hamilton said crisply. "Be alert for stationary men. Since the hour is late, most of the Society will be abed."

"Is it possible they don't even know we've escaped?" Dr. Mason asked.

"What did you do with the guard you subdued?"

Waverly's smile flashed. "He's bound hand and foot with that excellent sail cloth. I left him on the bottom floor of the warehouse."

"The first time anyone goes to see about us," Dr. Frank said with a wry grin, "they'll find their man."

"Or if they go searching for the sentry," General Waverly said.

"It is therefore my supposition that they will not be aware of your escape until tomorrow morning," Hamilton said.

Mrs. Conner asked, "How long will it take your 'people' to reverse the experiment, Dr. Mason?"

"I wish I knew, madam. This exchange was not planned. I have no idea what went wrong or how long it will take to put it right. But the reverse exchange can take place only in Dr. Franklin's house."

"There!" General Waverly said in a harsh whisper. "At the corner of that brick wall, see him?"

"Yes, General, I see him," Hamilton said. "What would you have us do about him?"

"Ask Mr. Bandry to slow further once we turn the next corner. I will step from the coach and take out the sentry."

"'Take out' is also unfamiliar to me, but I believe I instantly deduce its meaning. Kindly refrain from killing him, please"

"I won't. But I may leave him with a mild concussion."

Hamilton tapped the coach wall over the panel and, when Bandry responded, transmitted the instructions. The coach cornered and then slowed to a crawl.

"I'll meet you at Dr. Franklin's in ten minutes," General

Waverly said, slipping out into the night.

"My word!" the man dressed as Teddy Roosevelt exclaimed. "If it isn't three of the founding fathers." His forehead blazed with two fresh lipstick stripes and the smudged remains of two others.

"You have me at a disadvantage, sir," Franklin said. "I know you not."

"Bully. I am Theodore Roosevelt, twenty-sixth president of these United States." He regarded Franklin closely and then turned to Washington and Madison. "A successor to these worthy gentlemen. You know, I don't know you men, but these costumes are incredible. What year are you ostensibly from?"

"1787, May," Madison said.

"Ah, before the Con-, no, the convention to amend the Articles of Confederation." Teddy Roosevelt smiled widely. "So you all are delegates here in Philadelphia. What brings you to our humble party?"

"Miss Malone, obviously," Franklin said with a matching smile. The two men laughed together.

Teddy Roosevelt turned to Washington, held out his hand. "General, I am honored to meet you, sir. 'Father of Our Country' and all that."

Washington frowned down at the proffered hand before reluctantly shaking it. "What is your meaning, sir?"

"Well, upon your death-"

"Mr. Roosevelt," Annie said sharply, "the general is before you, act accordingly."

"Quite, quite. So sorry. You know, your impersonation of Washington is so authentic, right down to the glacial standoffishness. I'm quite awed."

"Thank you, but you see, I am George Washington."

"Of course you are. Tell me then, I've always wondered what it was like at Braddock's defeat."

"Braddock was a fool who thought everyone should make war by European rules. By fighting them in formation, he squandered his men as if they were shillings easily replaced. The regulars under his command were slaughtered like cattle.

"It took all of my energy to organize a fighting retreat and save what of the army we could." Washington's nostrils flared and the tempo of his breathing increased. "Had we not held our own on the retreat to Albany, it would have been known as Braddock's Massacre. You help me recall my youth, sir. For that I thank you."

Roosevelt turned to Annie. "Where did you find them, Miss Malone? They're incredible."

Annie urged her party farther into the room. "You wouldn't believe me if I told you. Let's just say you won't trip them up on questions pertaining to their era."

"Extraordinary," Roosevelt said. He turned to the visitors. "And you're James Madison…"

Their arrival attracted other members of Phi Alpha Theta. Individuals impersonating George Armstrong Custer, Malcolm X, Mark Twain, and Sitting Bull wandered up. All bore lipstick stripes.

Annie made introductions.

"Aha, fresh blood to trip up," Twain said.

"Founding Fathers," sneered Malcolm X. "And two of them owned slaves."

"It is an unfortunate state of affairs," James Madison said. "And it does not settle easily on my conscience."

"But you never gave them up during your lifetime," X said with a note of triumph.

"I don't know, my life is not yet over," Madison said in a whisper.

"Oho, sticking to your scripts quite well!" Twain all but shouted.

"They are quite convincing, visually," Custer said, scratching at his fake beard. "I've never seen three actors who more looked their parts. Where are you fellows from?"

Washington stepped forward and steadily held the three with his steel-gray eyes. "Mr. Madison and I are from Virginia. Dr. Franklin is from Pennsylvania." He turned to Annie. "Perhaps this is not the situation you envisioned, Miss Malone?"

"Hey, don't take me wrong," Custer said. "I think you guys look great. How about a drink?"

"Beware of white men offering you firewater," Sitting Bull said. "But then, you gentlemen were into that, too, weren't you?"

X held his ground in front of Madison. "How can you profess you believe in equality and still own other humans?"

Madison swallowed. "It is a deplorable institution, I freely admit it. You are a freedman, then?"

Franklin leveled his gaze at Sitting Bull. "I assure you, sir, I have never given a savage hard spirits."

"Perhaps not, Dr. Franklin. But I'm sure many of your contemporaries more than made up for your lack."

"Freedman!" X shouted, spilling half his drink. "You bet yo' white ass I'm a freedman! What the hell you think the Civil War was about?"

"Mike!" Annie said. "Cool it, they're from a different era, they don't know about anything that happened after 1787."

"It's Malcolm X to you, white girl. I'll give them points for staying in character, but they legislated the suppression of my people. That's why the Nation of Islam is so important because whites still want to see the black man in chains."

Annie frowned at him. "Are you finished?"

Malcolm X blinked, took a sip of the beer he held. "Yeah, I kinda got into it, didn't I? And I was out of character from the beginning, Muslims don't drink alcohol."

"What tribe are you from, Chief Sitting Bull?" Franklin asked.

"The Teton Sioux. Your people didn't know about us in your time. But later they waged a war of genocide against us."

"Genocide? I know not the term," Franklin said, frowning.

"It means, 'to kill off an entire race.'"

"But many tribes in my time are doing the same to us."

"So when in 1787 are you supposedly from?" X asked Madison.

"May 13th. Tomorrow we are gathering to amend the Articles of Confederation."

"No, you're not," Malcolm X said.

"Mike, I mean, Malcolm!" Annie blazed. "They really want to stay in character. Don't tell them anything that is going to happen in their future."

"Gonna be kind of a one-sided party, ain't it?"

"You can't trip them up on their characterizations if the event happened before May 13, 1787. Go ahead, try it."

Sitting Bull held Franklins gaze. "Just as the English would have done if any of the American Indians tried to take London over because they didn't like the way the English were using it. That's what happened in this country."

X interrupted, "Okay. There is something I always wanted to ask Dr. Franklin."

Franklin squared his shoulders and pursed his lips. His ample stomach rose and then dropped again when he immediately relaxed. "Here I am, ask away."

"As a member of the Hellfire Club did you sacrifice cats and debauch young virgins?"

Franklin's face went ashen and he staggered, nearly falling. Washington grabbed his arm to steady the old man, and glared at Malcolm X/Mike. "What a scurrilous question, sir. I am inclined to challenge you to a duel. Mayhap more than one of you." His eyes held those of Sitting Bull for a moment.

Malcolm X/Mike stepped back, his eyes wide with shock. "Hey, man, be cool. It's an honest question."

"It's just a party," Sitting Bull murmured.

Franklin accepted a glass thrust into his hand and gulped some wine that caused him to cough. The group near the door stood silent while the party chattered and laughed behind them.

"Perhaps there is somewhere else we could go?" Madison asked. "This, ah, situation, seems ripe for disaster."

"Wait," Franklin said in a strained voice. "He asked me a question for which there is an answer."

"Dr. Franklin," Washington said, "You are under no obligation to open yourself to scandal."

"Since we arrived here," Franklin said. "We have been constantly referred to as 'Founding Fathers' by our hosts. This indicates that we truly did create a wondrous thing in the spring of 1787, even though it still lies, hopefully, in our collective future."

"Man, these guys are great!" Custer muttered. "I've never seen anyone stay in character to that degree."

Franklin continued, "Just as in our era we have nearly deified many of the Greek and Roman philosophers and scientists, I suspect we have received the same sort of hide bound reverence in this era. Those Greeks and Romans were men with appetites just as I have always been a man with appetites. For some time now my palate has been rather spare." He chuckled and took another sip of wine.

"But during my middle years I sought fleshly excess. And, yes, I found it as a member of the Hellfire Club in London. I tell you this only to illustrate my existence as a man as well as a 'Founding Father' or whatever else may have been made of my few accomplishments."

"Was I correct," Malcolm X/Mike said, "…about what went on there?"

"Mike!" Custer and Mark Twain yelled in unison.

Franklin smiled. "We all took a vow of silence, and I shall keep it."

"I have a question," Madison said with a glance at Annie. "Under the rules stated by Miss Malone, I cannot ask specifics of my future actions. But I would inquire as to results. Specifically; has the eras since ours profited from the actions taken here in Philadelphia in 1787?"

"Without a doubt," Mark Twain said. "Not just this era but those in the past, and I dare say, future eras."

"That's speculation," Malcolm X said. "At least the future stuff. But, yes, Mr. Madison, what began there has blossomed into a republic that has the means to evolve while still adhering to the original principles set down in-"

"Mike, please don't say any more," Annie said.

"Would you lighten up, girl? You act like these guys are the real thing."

"Well," a sultry voice exclaimed, "who are these antiques?"

Franklin brightened while Washington frowned. Annie turned to behold a buxom young woman with long blonde hair. Her more-than-generous breasts, quivering with every movement, threatened to burst from her skimpy dress.

"Who the hell are you supposed to be?"

"You're too young to remember Mae West," the blonde said in a purring tone. A large contingent of males representing history from Caesar through John Kennedy followed in her wake.

"Mae West was an actress," Annie snapped.

"I notice you're the only one complaining," she drawled.

"Pray tell," Franklin said, "in what momentous events have you participated?"

"Why, honey, I'm a momentous event. Actress of stage, screen, and television, and legendary lover."

"Televis-" Franklin blurted, eyebrows at full arch.

Custer bent next to him and whispered, "would you like to see television?"

Franklin turned to him and whispered back, "Very much so, sir!"

"Come with me," Custer said and pulled Franklin by the arm.

"Were you a celebrated harlot, madam?" Washington asked. "With many men in your life?"

Mae smiled. "Why, honey, everybody knows is isn't the men in my life that's important, it's the life in my men."

Most of the crowd laughed, including Franklin as he followed Custer into the other room. Washington squared his shoulders and turned away, muttering, "Waste, sloth, immorality. This is what we became?"

Standing behind him, Annie heard him clearly.

Benjamin Franklin dropped onto a footstool before a box holding a man speaking in tones of authority. He looked up at Custer.

"Who is that man?"

"Don't tell Annie I told you, but that's the vice president of the United States." He smirked.

The man on the screen smiled and said, "And without further ado it is my very great pleasure to introduce the President of the United States, Barack Obama."

"Y'know," Custer said pulling on his arm, "I think I should get you back into the other room."

"If you insist," Franklin said staring back at the device.

"Annie can be hell on wheels, and she happens to be my academic advisor. I don't want to piss her off, know what I mean?"

"Perhaps," Franklin said.

"We gotta go now," Annie said, glancing at her watch. "We have an appointment."

"On a Sunday evening"? Twain asked with a knowing wink. "You can't just bring these fascinating people here and then leave without allowing everyone to enjoy them. They're really good at this."

Custer and Franklin edged back into the group.

Mae West tickled Franklin's chin. "And this one's cute!"

"Yeah," Custer said to Annie. "What do you want, money?"

"Guys, I really can't explain right know, we're running out of time in more ways than one."

"Where have you been lately?" Malcolm X asked.

Annie turned to her charges, motioning to Nick who firmly urged Franklin toward the door.

"Gentlemen, we have to keep our appointment."

Franklin touched Sitting Bull on the arm. "I never considered the situation from the aspect you presented me. But know that many of our governing principles were derived from, among other places, the Iroquois Confederation."

Malcolm X offered his hand to Franklin. "You're something else. I almost believe you are the real McCoy. I meant no disrespect, you know. Benjamin Franklin was an incredibly complex man, and you have him down to the nth degree, congratulations." He quickly turned to Madison and Washington.

"You gentlemen are also superbly well drawn. I wish I were as good at Malcolm X as you are at your characters. I'd love to rap with you again some time."

"The very next time we visit," Franklin said. "I promise."

Philadelphia - 1787

General Waverly quietly closed on the man leaning against the brick wall. Not for the first time during this strange evening he keenly regretted the lack of trees and bushes here in the center of town. The street seemed to abut the buildings.

Which no doubt accounts for the shutters on every window, he thought. This strange turn of events made him feel young again. For the first time in years he felt like a real soldier rather than a paper-shuffling administrator.

He would never admit to his fellow travelers how much enjoyment this adventure had brought him. Part of his pleasure stemmed from the fact that the Society of the Cincinnati fellows didn't seem to realize they were up against a worthy foe. Not smart to underestimate the enemy, he thought.

Three steps from the sentry, General Waverly raised his heavy pistol to strike. The sound of a flintlock hammer cocking to his left loudly broke the silence.

"General Waverly, how good of you to come to us," Colonel Thiebaldt rasped. "Now we'll just wait for your friends to complete their carriage ride and then we'll all have a nice, long chat."

The ambient light glinted off the barrels of two muskets, one on either side of General Waverly. He silently cursed himself. No matter the cost to himself, he decided, these people would not recapture his friends.

He debated which armed man to attack. Both were about three yards away with Thiebaldt sauntering up in front of him, still prattling, "...thought we wouldn't come back to check on you and your friends, did you? We've realized you're much rarer game than that which we first hunted."

The man on Waverly's left edged forward slightly and became the target of choice. He knew those muskets were heavy.

Seventeen pounds of weapon if memory serves.

Both weapons now sagged slightly. Waverly tensed, working out the action in his mind. Let Thiebaldt take one more step and-

Steel clashed down on the musket to Waverly's right, knocking the weapon from the man's hands. Instantly Waverly threw himself at the man on the left, knocking the musket aside with his left arm and striking the man across the temple with the heavy pistol still in his right hand. Before the man hit the ground, Waverly whirled about to engage Thiebaldt.

Alexander Hamilton held Colonel Thiebaldt at sword's point. The colonel stood mute, his head back as the sword point lifted his chin.

"You skulk in the darkness like an assassin, Colonel," Hamilton said. "You prey on unarmed, innocent citizens to further your own nefarious schemes. Does there exist any law which would condemn me for ending your life this very instant?"

"I beg you, sir," Thiebaldt said in a strained tone.

"Don't bother," Hamilton snapped. "I will not kill an unarmed man. Not even one who uses bullies to carry out his wishes. You will leave this place and never again bother Dr. Franklin, General Washington, or any other person who enjoys the hospitality of this house. Do you understand me?"

"Y-yes."

"You bring dishonor on the Society of the Cincinnati. At our next meeting I will petition to have you and your cronies turned out of the organization. Keep in mind that I am also a lawyer. By attempting to kidnap General Washington, you have declared yourself an enemy of mine. This will be the only time I show you an iota of mercy."

The sword flashed down to Hamilton's side. "Collect your rapscallions and be away from here at once or I shall have your life's blood."

Thiebaldt and his remaining man hurried over to their moaning comrade on the ground. Thiebaldt reached for the fallen musket.

Hamilton said, "Bandry." and the coachman stepped from the shadows with a pistol aimed at Theibaldt's head.

Thiebaldt backed away and assisted in getting his man up and the three of them stumbled off into the night.

"Well done, Mr. Hamilton," General Waverly said. "You saved my neck for certain."

"When it looks too easy, it usually is," Hamilton said with a smile. "Bandry, go bring our guests to Dr. Franklin's now."

Bandry gave Waverly a wide smile and, with his arms full of captured weapons, disappeared into the darkness.

Hamilton sheathed his sword. "I was going to suggest that you precede us and draw them out. But then you did that all on your own. So we followed."

"I plead guilty to hubris. I made the mistake of underestimating my enemy. Things could have been very bad."

"Don't be too hard on yourself. You're a soldier and a brave man, those are worthy titles."

"You once had your men charge a British fortification with bayonets fixed to unloaded muskets, didn't you?" Waverly asked.

"You know about that?"

"I know a lot of things that I should have remembered before now."

The carriage rattled up and Mrs. Conner stepped down before Bandry could get off the driver's seat. She hurried over to them.

"Are you gentlemen all right?"

"Thanks to Colonel Hamilton, everything is fine," General Waverly said.

"Excellent, let us get in out of the night air." Mrs. Conner led the way to Franklin's door. "Oh, look what a mess those ruffians made," she said, lighting a lamp.

"Easily put to rights," Waverly said, picking up a chair and setting it against the wall. "We'll all help, right gentlemen?"

"Of course," Frank and Mason said together.

Alexander Hamilton, standing near the door with Bandry, cleared his throat. "Well, gentlemen and lady, we must be on our way."

Mrs. Conner hurried over to them. "Mr. Hamilton, we are all in your debt. I will apprise Dr. Franklin of your assistance and heroism tonight. I thank you from the very bottom of my heart."

Hamilton's pale cheeks glowed rosy again.

"It was nothing, Mrs. Conner. I am very happy to have helped."

"We couldn't have done it without you," General Waverly said.

"Quite so," Dr. Mason said.

Dr. Frank stood in front of Hamilton while indecision washed through him. He wanted so much to shake this man's hand. But he also knew the custom of shaking hands wouldn't come into vogue until 1801 when Thomas Jefferson initiated the custom at his inaugural ball. Dr. Frank remembered Hamilton and Jefferson were already political foes and would become outright enemies during Washington's two administrations.

"I am so honored to have met you, Mr. Hamilton, that words fail me."

Hamilton bowed. "The honor is mine, Dr. Frank. It strikes me that you gentlemen are the three wise men come to celebrate the birth of a nation, if I may use such an illustrious analogy. For, indeed, your very presence tells me that our endeavors here in Philadelphia are worth all the effort they may demand.

"There are so many questions I would like answered, but I also understand your unique situation. The temptation to play God must be nearly overwhelming."

"Oh, sir," cried Dr. Frank. "If you only knew!"

"Yes, well, I must be off. I wish you all success in your journey back to your home." Then he hurried out into the night.

Dr. Frank took a step toward the door. Dr. Mason grabbed his arm. "Get hold of yourself."

Dr. Frank jerked his arm from the other's grasp. "How would you feel if you had just seen Einstein walk out that door?" he snapped.

"Point taken. Actually, I would feel just as honored to meet the man who lives here. My word, we are actually cleaning up after Franklin, Washington, and Madison. Can you believe it?"

"I would if you'd do more to help," General Waverly said from across the room.

Mrs. Conner laughed. "You all are making this task a pleasure. I shall quite miss you when you return to your, time." She shook her head. "This is all so unbelievable, yet here I am, accepting it as commonplace."

"That's the way humans are," Dr. Mason said, carrying a pile of plates into the kitchen. "The first time something amazing occurs, it is taken as a miracle. After that, people just say, 'Oh, I've seen that before.'"

"I'm sure," she said, "that your daily lives would seem miraculous to me."

"If we could only tell you, dear lady," General Waverly said. "But we can't."

"Oh," said a voice from the door, "but you will tell me."

They turned to see the entry crowded with armed men led by a glowering Colonel Thiebaldt. He waved a saber. "With just a few words from any one of you three, I think my future will be secure."

"I'm sorry," Annie said, walking toward the car. "That got a bit out of hand."

"What does 'rap' mean?" Franklin asked.

Nick explained.

"What an interesting term. What an interesting era. What an interesting woman masquerading as Madam West."

Madison cleared his throat. "I notice that individual rights seem to be universal. Is that true?"

"Very much so," Annie said, unlocking the Volvo.

"How are your leaders chosen?

"We vote for them."

"We. Do women have the vote?"

"Yes. It took women over a century to get the vote. And therefore I vote in every election."

"We believe in an enlightened self-government," Madison licked his lips, "which assumes an educated and refined class of governors, or voters, if you will. To give uneducated, unproven men the vote flies in the face of common sense. And to give their wives an equal opportunity to elect leaders would only double the uneducated disparity."

Annie awarded him a sardonic smile. "Rest easy, Mr. Madison, the rich still run the country, they just go about it differently now."

Both Washington and Franklin avidly studied the passing scene as she drove. Madison stared toward the windshield but when Annie glanced at him in the rearview mirror she saw that he focused on infinity.

"Are you feeling ill, Mr. Madison?" she asked.

He blinked and glanced at the back of her head. "Yes, thank you. I was also mulling over the short conversation I had with 'Mike' back at the reception, and his condemnation of slavery strikes a distinct chord in my being. It also has brought an ache to my head, I fear."

"As soon as we get back to the lab, I'll give you something that will ease the pain." Annie smiled reassuringly into the rearview mirror, and instantly became sober when she saw the flashing red and blue lights behind them.

"Oh, damn!" she blurted. "We're getting busted."

Nick twisted around to look. "It's the PPD, not the MPs. That's good."

"I hope so," Annie said, rolling down her window as the Black policeman stopped next to her door. "Is there a problem, officer?" she asked sweetly.

"May I see your operator's license, miss?" He switched on a powerful flashlight and ran the beam over the other occupants. "Been to a costume party?" he asked.

"Yeah, the history honor society party over on campus," Annie said, handing him her license.

"Well, Miss Malone," the officer said after a quick glance at the license, "...we've been alerted by the U.S. Army that you and an accomplice have kidnapped three men-"

"Kidnapped! We haven't kidnapped anyone." Annie felt white-hot anger surge through her. "Let me guess," she snapped before the officer could finish his sentence, "...the person who called was Lt. Colonel Thiebaldt, wasn't it?"

"Uh," the officer scanned down the page in his hand. "Yes, that's who made the call."

Annie smiled up at him. "Did he mention any names? Or just three John Does?"

The officer bent down and peered into the car, first at Nick, then at the three visitors. "Do you gentlemen have some identification, please?"

Nick gave his driver's license to Annie who passed it to the officer.

"Colonel Thiebaldt mentioned you, too, Mr. Gordon. Now that leaves the three passengers," he said, looking into the car again.

"Like you said, my friends are in costume for a party, they all left their ID at home, that's why they're riding with me."

"Miss Malone," the officer said. "If you don't mind, I'd like to hear their side of this."

Washington leaned forward and, in his frostiest tone, said, "Miss Malone has given you naught but fact, constable. Had she played fast and loose with the truth I would have interrupted at once."

"Your name, sir?"

"I am General George Washington, United States Army, retired. And who might you be, constable?"

"I'm, it doesn't matter who I am." His voice suddenly carried an edge. "George Washington is your legal name?"

"It most certainly is."

The officer grinned. "You're the first white man I ever met by the name of Washington. And you really do look like the guy on the dollar bill."

Washington leaned back in his seat. Annie glanced at him in the rear view mirror. The general seemed lost in thought, his forehead furrowed and face wreathed with serious creases.

"You other two gentlemen, your names, please?"

"Benjamin Franklin, my good man, printer, philosopher, diplomat, and inventor."

The officer's squint increased. "I wasn't much on history, but I remember seeing your picture, too." He looked at Annie again. "If I didn't know better, I'd say they were the real McCoy."

"Officer, it's getting late-"

He leaned down and looked at Madison. "Well, you don't look familiar, what's your name?"

"James Madison, representative from Virginia. My friends and I are with Miss Malone of our own free will. Furthermore, we have been with her all evening and will attest that she has not impeded the movement of any other person during that time."

"You sound like a lawyer, Mr. Madison."

"I confess that I have studied law a great deal, constable."

The officer stood to his full height. After glancing at the two licenses in his hand he gave them back to Annie. "I'm very impressed with the quality of your friends' impersonations. And I find nothing illegal here. Sorry to have bothered you. Colonel Thiebaldt is going to have to talk fast to get out of a charge of false police reporting. That's a felony."

Annie had the car moving before the officer reached his vehicle. She tightly gripped the steering wheel to hide her shaking hands.

"Miss Malone," Franklin said, "how does the intense lantern the constable carried work?"

"Nick."

"Batteries," Nick said.

"Batteries?"

While Nick explained storage batteries Annie drove toward the Gernsback Institute. Exhaustion pressed down and she yawned. Can't take much more tonight, she thought.

"How do they infuse the batteries with such an excess of

electrical fluid?" Franklin asked. "Our Leyden jars could only hold enough to produce a spark or two."

Annie grinned, turned the corner, and slammed on the brakes. "Damn!" she spat.

Fifty feet in front of her sat a U.S. Army roadblock.

"You scurrilous dog!" Mrs. Conner yelled, swinging her broom up sharply and hitting Theibaldt's arm, smashing his saber against the head of the man beside him. Stunned by the heavy blade, the man reeled back into his fellows. Mrs. Conner swung a second time, raking the brittle straws of the broom across Theibaldt's face.

General Waverly knew this was their only chance to act. "Get them," he growled, and grabbing a three-legged stool he charged the knot of men in the doorway.

One of the men broke free and raised a pistol to strike at Mrs. Conner. General Waverly caught the man's arm in the legs of the stool and twisted violently. The man shrieked as his arm broke and he fell back, tripping two more armed bullies.

One of the falling men hit his head on a side table, knocking him senseless. Waverly snap-kicked the other man in the head, collapsing him on his companion. Colonel Thiebaldt, holding his face in his hands, stumbled toward the general.

Waverly swung the stool against the side of the colonel's head, dropping him in his tracks. He pulled back the stool to swing at the next man and found the doorway empty of conscious life. "Where'd they all go?" he said in a hoarse voice, trying to dampen the bloodlust surging through him.

"We've routed them, General," Mrs. Conner said in a satisfied tone. "What a magnificent warrior you are!"

"What is going on here?" someone thundered in a baritone voice.

Waverly looked up to see a man carrying a pistol standing in the doorframe. He pulled the stool back to swing at him but Mrs. Conner grabbed his arm. "No, General! This is the constable."

"Mrs. Conner," the constable said, doffing his hat. "Pray tell, what transpires here?"

Mrs. Conner looked down at Thiebaldt and kicked a grunt out of the unconscious man. "This piece of cow flop broke into Dr. Franklin's house, assaulted myself and these three men, took us prisoner-"

"Mrs. Conner," the constable held his hand up. "Colonel Hamilton apprised me of what happened earlier." He nodded at the heap of men on the floor. "Is Colonel Thiebaldt among the bested here?"

"This," Mrs. Conner kicked another grunt out of Thiebaldt, "...is he."

The constable turned toward the door before his grin fully formed. Waverly decided he liked the man. "Allen, Verley, give a hand here," he shouted. Two strongly built men filled the doorway.

In moments the four prisoners were gone, two groggily stumbling under their own power and the other two dragged like sacks of comatose trash.

The constable eyed Waverly. "You attacked armed men with a foot stool?"

Waverly grinned, and nodded at Mrs. Conner, "Had to, she had the broom."

"Gotta reverse course, folks." Annie turned around as decorously as she could. She shifted into first and glanced at the rearview mirror. Two soldiers jogged toward her, waving.

"Hang on!" She popped the clutch and with a shriek of tires they roared down the street

"I didn't know you could do that with a Volvo," Nick said, letting go of the safety handle over the door.

"You can't with the new electrics," she said, taking a corner with minimal braking.

"Damn!" Nick shouted, quickly grabbing the handle to keep from flying into Annie. "Tell me before you do that again!"

"I told you to hang on."

"Miss Malone," Washington said with a slight quaver in his voice, "Pray reduce your speed. Dr. Franklin has gone into a faint."

"Please hang onto him, General. We're almost to our destination. If I slow down now, they might catch up with us."

She abruptly turned again and they bounced down a narrow alley. The car lost speed and she turned off the lights. They slowed to jogging speed.

Nick peered out the back window. "Were they even following us?"

"I wasn't sure." She stopped and set the hand brake. "I'll be right back, all of you stay in the car."

Before anyone could inquire or protest she slipped out and walked rapidly toward the street, ten yards away. On the other side of the boulevard sat the Gernsback Institute. The windows of the Project suite blazed with light.

She detected no movement within. She wished she could use her cell phone, but that could destroy circuits Ruth might be making. Ruth was supposed to be there alone, rebuilding the motherboard. "As if they wouldn't guard her," Annie whispered to herself.

She carefully examined the street in both directions before sprinting across the pavement to stop next to the hedge bordering the lawn. Nothing moved. The heat of the day lingered and sweat swamped her armpits. Her heartbeat pulsed in her head and she opened her mouth to hear over her breathing.

Staying in the darkness between the swaths of light from the windows, she slowly crept up to the building. She edged to the closest window and looked inside as far as possible without illuminating herself. On the far side of the room Ruth worked at the TIA console.

Annie couldn't see the door from where she stood. Crouching over, she scurried toward the corner closest to the entrance. As she neared the light slashing out from the corner of the building she slowed to a creeping pace. Deciding to take another peek, she edged up to the last window along the wall, and peeked in.

Hands grabbed both her arms. She jerked backward in fear and shock, but couldn't break the iron holds on her. They pulled her into the light. One held both arms while the other stepped around to confront her.

"Calm down, Annie," Jerry Burdock said around the lump on his jaw. "We're not going to hurt you. Where are the visitors?"

"Where's your master, Thiebaldt?" she snapped.

"He's not my master, he's my commanding officer."

"Bull. If he told you roll over you'd be covered with grass stains and dog poop."

"Make this easy on yourself, Annie." Burdick's voice held genuine anguish, but she refused to acknowledge it. In the darkness behind Jerry she saw movement. Realizing it must be Thiebaldt and the other guard, her will to fight lessened.

"You're despicable, Jerry. It probably wouldn't matter to you if I were your mother; you'd still follow illegal orders."

"Nothing's going to happen," he said. "All this will be straightened out officially. The army deals with everything in its own way."

"There's a chapter in your regulations dealing with time travelers?" George Washington loomed out of the darkness and his round house punch took Jerry completely unawares. At the same moment she heard a soft "thud" behind her and the grip on her arms melted away.

Annie's knees went weak with relief and she nearly fell. Strong hands caught her, pulling her out of the light. "Did they hurt you?" Nick Gordon whispered in her ear.

"No. I'm just a little tired." She let him support her fir a moment, realized his arms felt good. She forced herself to stand. "Hey," she hissed, "didn't I tell you guys to stay in the car?"

"Who said you were running the show?"

George Washington moved next to them. "Silence. We still

don't know the whereabouts of Thiebaldt and his other confederate. But they are not within."

"Are you sure of that?" Annie said.

"Absolutely."

"Great. Then I'll just walk in. If nothing happens, I'll open that window and Nick can go get Dr. Franklin and Mr. Madison while the General keeps watch. Okay?"

Washington and Nick regarded each other for a long moment.

"I can't find anything wrong with that," Nick said.

"Nor I," Washington agreed.

"By the way," she reached over and kissed Nick on the cheek, "thanks for saving me." Then she turned and walked into the light.

The four sat at the table of Dr. Franklin, eating his food.

"I can't remember being this hungry, even as a kid," General Waverly said.

"I confess to having been somewhat peckish," Dr. Mason said, pushing away an empty plate and patting his paunch. "But not any more."

Dr. Frank pushed his plate aside and leaned on the table. "How are they going to get us back, Dr. Mason?"

"I've been giving that a great deal of thought. They must recreate the incident."

"What exactly happened?" General Waverly said. "I mean I know that we stumbled into each other and hit the array. But why weren't we electrocuted, why didn't we just short out the field?" He waved his hand at the room. "How did we get here?"

Mason frowned, began slowly. "We like to think there's nothing about physics we don't know. When Nick Gordon proposed his quantum physics and electromagnetic mongrel hypothesis, I thought he'd gone off the deep end."

"I ridiculed him, told him he was wasting my time. I looked over his work, I'm his advisor, after all. But his theories seemed preposterous, like nothing I'd ever seen before."

"But they worked," General Waverly said. "How?"

Mason's face went red. "That's what I'm trying to say: I don't know."

"It takes a big man to admit he's been wrong," Dr. Frank said.

"I'm not looking forward to admitting it to Nick Gordon," Dr. Mason said with a laugh.

"I just hope you get the chance," General Waverly muttered.

"Well," Dr. Mason said, "We're in the right place if they reverse the process. I just hope they haven't already tried and failed."

"Is there any way we can tell from here?" Dr. Frank asked.

Dr. Mason looked around the room. "I, I don't know. I don't think so." He rubbed his face.

"There's something we haven't discussed, gentlemen." General Waverly's bass voice conveyed great gravity. "What happens if this situation is irreversible?"

Dr. Mason nodded at Mrs. Conner, "Then we'll have to invent

a reason for this fine lady to have us as guests in Dr. Franklin's home for as long as we last."

"Think again," Dr. Frank said. "Dr. Franklin, as well as General Washington and Mr. Madison, all disappear and we're here with no connection to this place and time? These people may not be as technologically sophisticated as we are, but they're damn well not stupid."

"Hell," General Waverly said, "for my money they're a lot smarter."

"I concur," Dr. Frank said. "We're going to have our work cut out for us to keep from being incarcerated, let alone lead any sort of worthy lives."

Mrs. Conner cleared her throat. "Gentlemen, I realize you come from a place I cannot begin to understand. But, if you, or your people, can bring you here, cannot they return you to your own time?"

General Waverly put his hand on hers. "You must understand, dear lady, this was the result of an experiment. We have no guarantee that it can be duplicated, ever."

Her face went ashen. "Then the desires of the Society of the Cincinnati might well come to fruition."

"Which brings up something unpleasant I've tried to not think about," Dr. Mason said.

"But obviously you have," General Waverly said. "What?"

"Okay, this gets a bit convoluted but let me try to explain." Dr. Mason gave both his colleagues a meaningful stare before continuing. "We are in the time of our grandparents, six or seven times removed. We don't belong here."

"It took you how long to come to this conclusion?" Dr. Frank snapped.

"Don't interrupt, dammit! This has never happened before, and I'm not sure that the laws of physics will allow it to happen now."

"Dr. Mason," General Waverly said, "it has already happened. This situation is fact."

"But for how long? I think that we will experience a, for lack of a better term, a time erosion."

"Time erosion?" Waverly and Frank blurted in unison.

"What exactly does that mean?" Dr. Frank asked.

"I think that we, and everything we brought with us, will be expelled from this continuum. We may not survive the experience."

"How much of that beer did you drink?" General Waverly asked.

"Porter," Mrs. Conner corrected absently.

"And you thought Nick's thesis was preposterous?" Dr. Frank said with a laugh. "What do you base your theory on?"

Dr. Mason seemed close to tears. He stared hard at the general. "Okay, where's your uniform?"

"I changed into these clothes that Mr. Hamilton gave us, you know that."

"But we brought our own clothing with us," Mason persisted. "Where are they?"

"In the jute sack," Mrs. Conner said, "…there by the door."

"Show me."

After a quizzical look, she retrieved the sack and held it up. "Right here, sir."

"Dump it on the floor," he said in a flat voice.

She upended the sack and buttons and insignia from General Waverly's uniform jacket hit the floor and bounced, followed by three metal belt buckles.

"Dr. Mason whined deep in his throat. "Damn, I was right."

"I don't understand," General Waverly said. "Where's my uniform?"

"I really don't know," Dr. Mason said. "But it's been expelled from this time."

"But the buttons…" Dr. Frank said, "…are still here."

"They have more mass, is my theory, just as we do."

"How'd you know?" General Waverly asked.

"I wanted to put on my own shirt, this one is scratchy. When I looked in the bag I actually saw it disappear."

"But, but what about our underwear?" Dr. Frank mirrored Dr. Mason's agitation. "I know mine is still on."

"Yeah, mine too," agreed the general.

"Like I said, we have the most mass. Our underwear is being held in stasis by our bulk. I think we'll, ah, last longer if we stay together. But I don't think our situation is permanent."

"Just as well," General Waverly said. "As much as I like you gentlemen, I don't want to spend the rest of my life in the same room with you."

"That may be a shorter time than you think," Dr. Mason said with a growl.

"I hope Annie, Ruth, and Nick can fix this, and fast," Dr. Frank said.

"Yeah," General Waverly agreed. "Or history is going to lose us, not to mention three founding fathers."

Annie walked through the door and closed it quietly. Ruth sat hunched over the workbench, wearing magnifying glasses, intent on her project.

"Are we there yet?" Annie asked.

Ruth started, jerked around to face her while ripping the glasses off. "Annie! How did you get here? How did you get past them? They've-"

"Ruth! It's been crazy, but we're okay. Have you fixed the motherboard yet?"

"Oh, God, thank God. I was so worried. Yes, I've even built another one as backup, just to keep busy. We're ready to go."

Annie hugged the older woman. "Great, you're wonderful. I'll go get the guys."

"Guys?" Ruth said as Annie hurried out.

Franklin and Madison arrived at the shaded corner the same time Annie did.

"Come on," she whispered. "Ruth says we're ready to try it again."

They all followed her back into the lab. Annie held the door and, as Nick followed the other three past her, slammed it shut and locked the knob button as well as shooting the deadbolt.

"Good thinking, Annie," Nick said.

"You help Ruth," she said, "while I go lock the back door."

Nick nodded and went to confer with Ruth. The three visitors looked about.

"How are we to effect this incredible journey?" Franklin asked.

"Remain calm," Washington said. "They'll tell us."

"All of this has hardened my resolve that the military not be allowed to control our nation," Madison said. "We must guard the rights of the citizens."

Annie hurried back into the room. "Gentlemen, please have a seat."

They sat together and looked at her expectantly.

"Okay, once they have the TIA up-"

"TIA?" Franklin said, eyes full of curiosity.

"Temporal Information Array," she explained. "We didn't think it was going to do anything more than let us view the past."

"What will you call it now?" he asked.

"Doesn't matter. Okay, when I say 'now', the three of you hold hands and one of you, General Washington please, touch the array here." They watched solemnly as she tapped the metal mesh.

"What will happen then?" Washington asked.

"Well, when General Waverly touched it he and the two professors went somewhere and you came here. There are no guarantees, this may not work."

"But there are no alternatives, correct?" Madison asked.

"No, sir, there are no alternatives."

"Miss Malone," Franklin said, I must have a word alone with you."

"Okay, but we have to make it fast." She led him away from the others. "What is it, Doctor?"

"You must answer me two questions, it is very important."

"What two things?"

"The president of the United States is the highest position in this nation, yes?"

She glanced around, and then gave him a level stare. "Yes, that is true."

"And, and the current President of the United States is a black man?"

"How did you–," she swallowed and looked him in the eyes. "Yes. That's true."

"We must not let my companions know that," he said with a smile, "…else we might negate this incredible future of yours!"

She grinned and hugged him quickly. "I agree. Now get back to your friends."

Nick flopped down in his chair, fingered his keyboard and yelled, "Let's do it!" Annie moved behind him and watched, her hands on his shoulders.

Ruth and Nick began their choreographed movements. The overhead lights dimmed and the cutting odor of ozone grew strong.

Wham! The loud bang on the door made everyone jump.

"I order you to open this door!" came the muffled shout.

"Thiebaldt," Washington said, rising to his feet with a glint in his eye.

"Keep going!" Annie said. "Don't worry, General, they can't get in."

The huge mesh began to glow bluely.

"Everything's working," Nick crowed. "You did a beautiful

job, Ruth!"

"Thanks, I tried to think of everything."

A much louder slam rattled the door, another, and another.

"They've got a sledgehammer, Annie," Nick said. "We've got to hurry."

The mesh crackled into a low hum that rapidly gathered strength. Annie tried to remember the sequence from before, but so much had happened it seemed like a hundred years ago.

The slams worked into a rhythm and the door rattled looser and looser with each successive blow.

"Hurry, Nick!" Annie whispered, then bit her lip. She knew he and Ruth were moving as quickly as possible.

The glow suddenly flashed to the top of the mesh on all four sides and snapped together in an instant across the top. Nick moved his fader switch and the high whine eased into an angry-bee hum.

"This is fantastic!" Franklin said. Washington and Madison nodded in wide-eyed fascination.

The mesh cage went from blue to transparent and a scene took shape.

"Oh, no!" cried Annie. "There's a woman with them, we don't want to bring her here."

"Mrs. Conner," Franklin said.

The door smashed inward and crashed loudly on the floor. Lt. Col. Thiebaldt rushed into the room.

"That's it," he shouted. "Cease all activity at once!"

"Do you smell something?" Dr. Frank said.

His three companions all raised their heads and sniffed.

"Ozone?" General Waverly said.

"Ozone!" Dr. Mason leaped out of his chair. "It's them, they're getting though or we wouldn't smell anything."

"Where?" Mrs. Conner said, twisting her head back and forth.

"We have to get her out of here," General Waverly snapped, "or she'll go with us." He stood and pulled her out of her chair. "You have to go away from us, over by the door."

"You're leaving. Oh, sir, it has been such an excitement!" Mrs. Conner grabbed his head and kissed him hard on the lips. She broke away and raced across to the door. She smiled at him, her hands clasped over her bosom.

"Nothin's happening," Dr. Frank said. "Maybe it isn't going to work."

"You cur!" Washington shouted and in a bound he confronted Thiebaldt, who suddenly realized his position.

Before Jerry and the other soldier behind the Lt. Colonel could do anything, Washington punched Thiebaldt in the side of the head, knocking him back against the two men.

"The woman is leaving the room!" Annie shouted. "They know we're trying it."

"I can't hold this much longer!" Nick wailed. "Do it."

Thiebaldt lay on the floor, unconscious. Jerry and his comrade scrambled to their feet and fled back through the door.

"General," Annie shouted, "you have to go now!"

He turned and raced back to his peers, grabbing Franklin's hand. Madison and Franklin already gripped one another. Washington glanced back at the room.

"Thank you for a most interesting evening, Miss Malone."

Behind him, Benjamin Franklin gave her a lascivious wink.

George Washington touched the mesh and a bright blue glow crackled and encompassed the three men. Bathed in the strange light all three visitors smiled at their hosts while their bodies seemed to lose substance.

The main power cord burst into flame. The breaker box blew with a bang and instantly stank of burned metal. The room went black.

"Did it work?" Annie said into the darkness.

A powerful flashlight snapped on from the direction of Ruth's console, played across the wide floor.

Three figures struggled to their feet. Annie's heart nearly stopped when she saw they wore long stockings and short pantaloons.

"My God," General Waverly said with a sigh. "What a trip."

Nick reset the breakers and turned on the overhead lights.

"What happened here?" Dr. Mason said, pointing at the door.

"Colonel Thiebaldt wanted to be a nobleman," Annie said. "I just hope he hasn't succeeded."

"You mean Lieutenant Thiebaldt," General Waverly growled looking around. "If he even gets to keep his uniform."

Dr. Mason walked over to Nick. "There's a place for you on the faculty if you want it, Doctor Gordon."

"Did you actually talk to them, Annie?" Dr. Frank asked.

"Oh, yeah. We even took them to a party."

"You must write a full narration for me, please?"

"Happily, but not tonight." She glanced through the door at the strengthening daylight. "Not this morning, that is."

"It is imperative that we speak of this to no one," George Washington said.

"I completely agree," Madison said.

"Yes," Franklin said with a sigh, "I concur."

"But, General Washington," Mrs. Conner said, "what of Colonel Thiebaldt? He knows everything."

"Washington's eyes looked bleak. "I'll deal with the colonel, fear not."

"But it was so splendid," Franklin said.

Annie looked up from her meal in the commons as Nick approached with his tray. "Hi, lover."

He grinned and kissed her before sitting down. "You look happy. Decided to move in with me?"

She laughed. "Not so fast, buster. A girl's has to be sure of her man before she makes a commitment like that. But I do have some interesting news."

Nick bit into his grilled cheese sandwich, raising his eyebrows. "Hmm?"

"I went back through the Early National Period collection, I just had to know."

"Know what? We already figured out that nothing changed."

"Theibaldt's great-whatever grandfather. Dr. Frank told me he was as big a pain in the butt as our version was."

"Oh, what about him?"

"He spent the last part of his life in an insane asylum."

Nick shrugged. "I guess if you run around talking about visitors from the future, at some point they're going to lock you up."

The genesis of this story goes back to AlasKon, the only speculative fiction convention ever held in Alaska, in 1991. Mike Armstrong talked the University of Alaska into sponsoring it and UA in its infinite wisdom decided it was like any other symposium and charged way too much for attendance. As a result there were very few of us there.

The invited speaker list was incredible: Nancy Kress, Kristine Katherine Rusch, Dean Wesley Smith, Ed Bryant, and Chris Claremont in addition to every member of SFWA in Alaska (including me). One of the panels was about world building and we came up with the idea of a mostly water world.

That's when the concept of this story hit me. I made notes and when I got back to Juneau, wrote the story. The late Algis (AJ)

Budreys bought it for his (then) print magazine, *TOMORROW, Speculative Fiction,* and it appeared in Issue 12 in 1994 under the title, *WHEN THE SHIP CAME.* Now, twenty-one years later, it is back in print under my original working title.

AlasKon was the first science fiction & fantasy convention I ever attended and was the most memorable. Thanks, Mike!

Tabu

The profanity lay in perfect execution. Entrails webbed out across the smooth wooden deck. Pegged down with a still-green sawthorn, the sacrifice pointed stiff appendages to the four corners of the world, forming a mockery of the sacred sign.

Samit slowly scratched his bristly jaw while he pondered at the true meaning in the mess of feathers and guts. His bare toe touched the small rib cage.

Colder than the deck.

After noting the nuances of the splayed bird, he pulled the sawthorn out of the center. This seemed more sedition than blasphemy. A practiced kick sent the wasted meat splashing into the calm water between four-ring and three-ring of the great raft.

"You didn't see this until your last patrol?" he asked the silent guardsman.

"No sir. Large Moon set early and Small Moon is coming up right behind Jael. For about three spans it was very dark. I didn't want to kindle a torch…"

"You were correct to waken me… Avik, isn't it?"

"Yes, sir!" he replied, obviously pleased. "Guardsman First Class."

"Don't mention this to anyone else, Avik. Carry on, guardsman."

The first direct rays of Jael rose above the eastern horizon as the man hurried off to complete his morning patrol.

Samit carried the star-metal-tipped staff of the Maa, his symbol of office. On occasion it also proved to be a formidable weapon.

With daybreak the people of Concordia began to stir out of their wooden abodes. Women called to sleeping children. Kitchen noises issues from all directions.

The morning breeze carried the odor of frying weedcake, causing his stomach to grumble. Crossing the last catwalk to the bridge deck brought him into view of the Capin's sentry. The Maa smiled beneath his heavy mustache as the young guardswoman stiffened to attention.

"Anything to report?" he asked softly.

"No, sir!" she piped. "All is quiet."

"Your relief will be here soon." He pushed past her flat, "Sir," and edged through the door. Another armed guardswoman confronted him in the narrow passageway.

"The Capin still sleeps, Maa Samit," she said politely.

"My apologies and regrets, but I must speak to her as soon as possible."

The young woman inclined her head smartly. "Yes, sir. If you'll wait in the duty office I'll awaken her."

Samit wearily walked across the antechamber and dropped his bulk onto a padded bench.

My years are beginning to show.

The thought carried coldness with it, reminiscent of north drifting.

Capin Jeen padded barefoot into the room, tying the belt of her soft-cloth robe. Samit stood abruptly and gave her an abbreviated salute.

"Good morrow, Maa Samit," she said with a wave of her hand. "You have a need to see me?" She slid behind the desk of polished blackwood and settled in her chair, eyes alert.

"Please sit."

Samit slouched into a comfortable position. "A sacrifice was found this morning, just before dawn."

"Sacrifice? What kind of sacrifice?"

"Chicken. Expertly done, too."

"This isn't Bellday. Have you asked the Cassock about it?"

"No. The sacrifice was on the deck in front of the North Chapel door, not inside."

"Oh." Her stern mask of command slipped for a blink, and he saw the uncertainty of youth flash and fade. "This is more serious than I thought. It's the heathens, isn't it?"

"Yes, he said softly, "I'm afraid it is."

"You... took care of it?"

"Yes, Capin Jeen."

"Good." She chewed her lower lip. "Those of the new religion are getting bolder, aren't they?"

"It would seem so. First was talk about wind-catchers, and now this. I think the small grease-fish harvest left too many with time on their hands."

He stretched. "Word on ten-ring has it that they're already fighting among themselves – a schism in the schism. In just two links we'll be in the midst of the red fish and there won't be idle time for heresy, or sedition."

"But that won't last forever. Do you think you can find the people behind this before we finish the red fish run? Breaking tabus shouldn't go unpunished."

"I'll do my best, capin."

"I know you will." Her sudden smile gave him a lift, which surprised him. "Will you break fast with me, Maa Samit? Bayrn is using the last of the dried flatfish in the weedcakes."

"My thanks and regrets. But my wife is expecting me right about now."

"Of course. Well then, until the return of the Ship."

"Until the return of the Ship," he said mechanically.

A new sentry patrolled the bridge deck catwalk. Her polished breastplate of evilfish leather reflected the morning sun as she saluted smartly. He hurried through the formal streets of two-ring and three-ring. Nobody loitered near the site of the sacrifice.

As he approached the maze of market stalls on five-ring, he slowed. Rani's standing order was to bring home a vegetable for evening meal if he could find something fresh. The aura of rich dirt and night soil permeated rings five, six, and seven – a reminder of human cycles and needs.

He stopped at a stall that displayed thick, purple-tipped flowers. Chickens cocked their heads and eyed him from a cage behind the proprietor.

"Good morrow, Maa Samit," the dirt-man said. He pointed to the vegetables. "These are fresh cut this very dawn. Only a tenth-piece each."

"Did you venture from five-ring before dawn, Famir?" Samit picked up two of the vegetables and peered at their stalks. Moisture still oozed from the cuts.

"Where would I go? I've more than enough to do right here on five-ring. I haven't been across a catwalk before noon in over a link-set. If you're not going to buy those, I'd appreciate it if you'd put them down."

"I'll buy them. Would you throw in some wrap-weed to keep them fresh?"

"Well, since it's you..." The dirt-man pulled the end of a broad, translucent sheet of wrap-weed up to counter level and deftly sliced off a length with his shell knife. As he wrapped the purchase he glanced up at the stocky Maa. "So was there something to see on another ring at dawn?"

Samit stared impassively back. "Not to my way of thinking."

Famir held out a callused hand. "Two-tenths, please."

Three children raced past, laughing and shrieking. Samit dug out the coins and dropped them into the waiting hand.

"Until the return of the Ship." He turned toward home.

"Yeah," Famir's voice floated after him, "until the return of the Ship."

Religion, Samit reflected, was becoming complicated on Concordia. Was Famir's response an indication of an impious man or was he part of the new religion? Names and faces had constantly flicked through his mind since finding the chicken.

He continually rejected the one name that stuck to his mental fingers every time he sifted it out. Lots of people raised chickens. At least it wasn't a goat; his penurious nature would have demanded the use of goat meat, even if its death were an act of rebellion.

Rebels: religious rebels, or just rebels? Why couldn't this happen on one of the other rafts or on one of the rich islands?

By the time he put foot on south five-ring the sun blazed down fiercely. Already the morning breeze had died down to a whisper that reached no farther into the floating city than seven-ring.

"Daddy!" Gordo crowed from the side yard. The small, golden-haired boy swarmed into Samit's arms. The Maa hugged his youngest child to him in heartfelt emotion.

"Mamma says that I get to sit next to you at breakfast because I was so much help today already!"

"You are a good boy. I will be honored to have you sit by me. Here, carry my staff into the house and put it away."

Gordo's eyes rounded as he bravely accepted the two-meter badge of office.

"You spoil that boy," Rani said from the stove with a twinkle in her eye. Samit stepped into the kitchen.

"That's what small children are for." He ran his hand down her back and patted her behind. "What gossip fills the air today?"

"Fear," she said, turning back to the stove. "Sit. Your breakfast is ready."

He watched her face as she served him. Sometimes it seemed she had always been by his side and not just for the past seventeen drifts. Over the long drifts she had thickened, become wrinkled, and gray flecked her hair.

By the same token, her constant love and affection had deepened and taken root in his soul. Five living children had issued from that body. Four still received nurturing when they needed it, no matter how busy her day. Jori was dead. Only Gordo shared the house with them.

"Fear of what?"

"Omens in the night sky. Growing beliefs about sacrificing to the drift, rather than to the Ship. Arguments over a great wind catcher for Concordia and guided destiny rather than one of drifting."

He swallowed his first bite of food. *This thing again!*

"Our people have drifted true since the death of the Ship. Why should we change now?"

"My husband," calm reproach flexed with in her voice, "you asked me what gossip came with the sun. I am telling you, not agreeing with it."

"I know that," he said shortly. "Sacrificing to the drift! What kind of omen?"

Rani stopped moving around the kitchen and sat across the thick table from him.

"Steaks of light in the night sky," she said evenly. "Very high up."

"Falling bits of star, like in my father's time." He took another bite of weedcake.

"This one didn't fall and make great waves. It scratched fire across the heavens from horizon to horizon, following the path of Jael."

Samit found it difficult to swallow his food. He drank tea before responding.

"You talk as if you saw this thing yourself."

"I did." Her eyes grew larger, almost capable of swallowing him.

"A dream?" he ventured, putting down the cooling food.

"No dream. I was awake, emptying my bladder. The night was warm and the stars seemed to call me." She swallowed. He thought she might have blushed slightly.

"You actually heard voices?"

"Of course not. It was lyrical, that's all I'm saying."

He bit off a nettled response, sipped tea, and stared into his carved cup as he set it down. "You were pissing and felt lyrical. Then what happened?"

"If you continue to be rude, I won't tell you anything," she said flatly.

His face burned beneath the stubble. Frustration at her sideways explanation was not a good reason to be short with her. There was a side to her that he still didn't understand. In their collective youth many arguments grew from his inability to perceive her nuances. Finally he had just decided to be as accepting as possible.

"I'm not trying to be rude. I just stated facts like a good investigator."

"You stated them rudely. I'm not a wind-catcher advocate who has urinated on the Capin's door. I'm your wife."

"I'm sorry I was rude, Rani," he said, dissipating his momentary anger.

"I watched the thing – it looked like small, bright bead – as it went overhead. It didn't frighten me. It made me feel like a child again, somehow."

"Why didn't you wake me?"

"By the time I thought of that, it was gone. Besides, you always get angry when I wake you for reasons you don't agree with." She pushed off her chair and rattled utensils at the stove.

"Which quarter of the night did this take place?"

"About a span before you were called by the guard. Was there anything unusual on the morning patrol?"

"Not in the sky." He took another bite of his now-cold weedcake.

"But there was something unusual?"

Briefly he told her of the blasphemous bird carcass in front of the chapel.

"Who would do such a thing?" she asked wonderingly.

"I've been asking myself the same thing since I saw it."

"Maybe somebody just doesn't like chickens, Daddy," Gordo said at his side. Samit had forgotten that the child was there.

"Maybe so, little man, but don't say anything to your friends about it, okay? We'll keep this a secret between the three of us."

"Sure, Daddy! Just like the other secrets."

"Yes. You're a good boy, Gordo."

Samit wondered yet again if he would have married if he had known he would become the Maa. The Maa had to appear to be a bit harder than ironwood, brighter than the noon sky, and as unswerving as the path of the drift. It was difficult to be part of the Maa's family.

Once there had been a deputy who had worked with him. However the man's wife, daughter to one of the rich fish-leather processors, had grander plans for her husband. She didn't like the constant, careful evasion of her neighbors over trivial matters they thought might stretch the laws of Concordia.

Between the social distance the community maintained, and the hours her husband spent at his obligations, enmity formed in her. Samit sighed at the memory. Darwayne would have made an excellent Maa in time, and it was the only high office that wasn't hereditary.

He hoped his old deputy was happy overseeing the tanning of evil-fish hide for his father-in-law. In more ways than one, the job smelled too much to ever suit Samit. "It's all in the drift," he muttered to himself.

"Did you say something?" Rani asked.

"If you see that light in the sky again, come and wake me."

"As you wish." She bent over Gordo and touched his head fondly. "Son, you need to hurry. The proctor will be starting her lessons shortly."

"Yes, Mamma," he said dutifully.

Samit felt constant amazement at the good nature of his youngest son. Maybe there was something in the old wives' tale that a man begets what he feels at the time. Gordo had been conceived in a state of quiet, tender lovemaking.

His oldest son had been a product of hot lust. Sticky bellies lunging at one another in youthful sexual exuberance, seed screaming to be planted between fecund thighs, had begat Ansul: the son who despised him. Samit again forced his mind away from the one name that kept coming up in his mental net.

Gordo skipped out the door to attend day-lessons at South School. Rani moved lightly across the room.

"Are you going to sleep now?" Her eyes were open pools of emotion. Samit felt a welcome familiar stirring.

"Yes. Would you like to lie down with me?"

Her smile answered.

"Samit! There's something in the sky, Samit. Wake up!"

He slapped at the insistent hand shaking his shoulder. "Stop it, needta sleep!"

"Samit!" Rani said roughly. "You are needed."

Discipline finally cleared his mind of sleep. He sat up and rubbed his gritty eyes.

"What's happening?" he asked calmly, concentrating on her voice.

"There's a guard at the door, the Capin wants you immediately. There's something in the sky."

"Well, why didn't you say that to begin with?" He leaped up and pulled on clothing.

"I did, you old fool," she said fondly.

"Where's my staff?" His blood began to thunder in his ears. Rani handed him the rod without comment.

He bolted from the house. For just a moment he searched the sky but saw nothing.

Then he moved quickly, following the guardsman toward the Bridge Deck.

"Make way!" shouted the sentry at the catwalk when she sighted Samit's staff. "Make way for the Maa!" The buzzing crowd parted, but some shouted questions.

"What is it, Samit?"

"Is it really the Ship?"

"Will everyone die now?"

"Was it wrong to believe in the drift?"

For a moment he spied Ansul's face, his moist, gleaming eyes staring opaquely at him, before the youth became lost in the crowd. The Maa pushed through the crowd without answering. What in the name of *Jihad* was happening?

Capin Jeen paced back and forth across her office. Cassock Wye flipped through his copy of the Holy Log with such unholy haste his jowls were bouncing.

"It speaks of transceiver settings and wave lengths! I have never understood any of these communications entries. I always thought they were holy mysteries!"

Samit paused for a moment to enjoy the sight of Wye losing control. Old convictions hardened, but this was no time to gloat. Besides, as Maa he had to pay lip service to the official religion.

He saluted Capin Jeen formally.

"You wanted to see me?"

She stopped pacing and stared at him with strange eyes. He realized she was as close to panic as the Cassock.

"Something," she gasped. "Flew. *Over* Concordia. Something very *big*. She controlled herself with great effort.

"A sea roc?"

"Not a bird. T'was shiny. It made a sound – didn't you *see* it?" she shrilled and resumed her pacing without waiting for an answer.

"No. I was sleeping. Where did it go?"

"Away!" She flung out an arm and shook her hand in the air. "I don't know where. I have the entire guard out watching for it. They'll sound the evilfish alarm if–"

A high whistle cut through the room. Cassock Wye burst into sobs and fled down a dark passageway. Samit ran toward the door.

Pandemonium swirled around the Bridge Deck. Four guardswomen with ironwood pikes kept the townspeople off the catwalk. In the tower above the bridge two guardsmen shouted and pointed at something Samit couldn't see.

He went up the nine-meter ladder as fast as his tired legs could carry him. Once at the top, he flopped wheezing onto the platform, willing away the dancing spots from in front of his eyes.

"Wh-what the swive is going on?" he gasped.

Both guardsmen stiffened to attention and saluted.

"Flog that! Tell me what's happening!" Samit pulled himself up to the top of the wooden shield.

"That flew over us some time ago. Now it's – back..." the guardsman broke off and simply stared.

Samit blinked, but it didn't go away. Then habit engaged and he studied the thing carefully.

Still a league away from outer ten-ting, the object seemed impossibly huge. It floated in the water ponderously, no, not just floating – it moved. It left a wake like a water bird.

Sunlight reflected off high black sides, flaring to brilliant specks when it caught on little round spots that looked like an orderly pox.

Metal, he decided, *it was made of metal. It had to be at least a hundred meters high.*

"This thing *flew* over Concordia?" he asked.

"Yes, Maa. It's completely round."

It edged steadily closer. He could discern small movement on the side of the thing. One of the round places suddenly opened to reveal at least three people standing inside the dark metal skin.

Samit involuntarily crossed index fingers in the holy sign. Of their own accord, the two guardsmen mirrored his action. Abruptly he realized that the metal flying-thing would come to rest at ten-ring, near East Chapel guard tower. Rapid flashes from the heliograph asked frantic questions concerning protocol.

Samit slid down the emergency post so quickly his hands and legs burned where they clasped the smooth wood. His feet slapped the deck, stinging, and he grabbed a guardswoman.

"Get me a ten-rank of armed guards. Unfurl the great banner. Fall in at the catwalk. Now!" He rushed into the Capin's quarters without looking back.

Capin Jeen sat at her desk, trembling. There was no sign of Cassock Wye.

"Get up!" he shouted, startling her. "It's some kind of ship, it has to be. It's floating on the water and closing on East Chapel tower. We have to meet it there."

"Meet it! Why?"

"Because you're the Capin! I'm the Maa. We're the authority here and the people must see us carry out our duties."

"But I'm scared, Maa Samit!" A tear ran down one cheek.

"So am I, Jeen," he said softly but with great force. "However this is our responsibility. Now please put on your best cape and don't forget your scepter. Please hurry, my Capin."

"Yes, Maa Samit." She hurried from the room.

The phalanx of guards quick-marched through East Chapel, screaming at the frenzied Concordians to clear the way. Capin Jeen trotted to keep pace with Samit and the soldiers. The frightened people shouted so many questions that babel reached the ear.

For over 300 years the faithful had ended discussions with, "Until the return of the Ship." *Jihad*, the Ship of legend, had come from Earth, a world where magic and machines did one's work, where food and time for pleasure abounded. *Jihad* touched down on Aquaria, was attacked by evilfish and destroyed.

Only hard work and strict obedience would bring the *Redeemer Ship*, the Cassock preached. Follow the Holy Word and the Ship would return. *Jihad* had called for help and if the people kept the fait, salvation would be theirs.

The small band of survivors came to be called First Crew. For

300 years most of the people of Aquaria worked hard and kept strong the faith that a ship would come, but none ever had.

Until now?

Each ring of Concordia measured one hundred meters from water channel to water channel. The three-meter channels served many purposes, most of them good. Ten rings made for a long walk when coming from Bridge Deck in the center of the raft city. A full kilometer must be crossed before they could greet the visitors.

Even the guardsmen and guardswomen stumbled winded, leaden by the time they hurriedly wound through the factories, and fish drying sheds of ten-ring.

"Hold the banner high, so they will know to whom they must speak," Samit ordered. At the unimpeded sight of the huge metal-flying thing, Capin Jeen's pace faltered even more.

"It will be all right," Samit said in a low voice, hoping he was correct.

"Y-yes, it will be all right," Capin Jeen echoed.

Her father shouldn't have died so young, Samit thought. *He should be here handling this, not her.*

Samit knew he needed to take charge and conduct the situation without allowing the people or the strangers on the – ship – to realize that Capin Jeen foundered.

They came to a stop at water's edge. The guard flanked the Capin and Maa in straight ranks, trying to look warlike with their leather armor and ironwood spears. Samit noticed that more than one set of knees shook despite the heat of the day.

He stared up and out at the great shape. Five people in identical clothing stood in the opened circle. Squinting to pick out more detail, he realized that both men and women stared back.

The thing stopped perfectly still in the water. A noise reminiscent of a coughing evilfish blurted from the opening. It made no sense.

"Galactic speaking, are you?" a great hollow voice asked. Some of the guard backed up in astonishment. Capin Jeen clapped both hands to her mouth.

"Yes?" Samit shouted. "We speak that language."

The newcomers conferred among themselves. This time Samit spotted the man who spoke.

"May we enter your city?" He didn't cup his hands or shout; yet his voice boomed out of the great metal orb like thunder in a spring storm.

Samit nudged Capin Jeen with his elbow. "Tell them, *yes*," he muttered.

"Do you think it wise, Maa Samit?" she asked in a trembling voice.

"Do you really think we could stop them even if we really wanted to?"

She looked up at the people in the large opening.

"We would be honored by your presence!" she said in a loud, clear voice. Samit felt proud of her.

"Thank you," the man said, his voice echoing away across the water.

A loud hum emanated from the opening and a thick tongue of metal suddenly protruded from the curved side and angled down toward ten-ring. Samit watched it move deliberately and smoothly through the air, without wavering or faltering, until it touched down on the wood in front of him with a solid *thunk*. Rails lifted out of each side of the ramp and clicked to a stop at waist level.

The ramp surface began to move. The strangers stepped on and moved down the thirty-meter distance while standing and looking around them.

Samit thought about the magic unfolding in front of him and decided this was how a waterlouse must feel when dropped onto a hot deck in front of men.

Outclassed, no comparison at all.

A tall gray-haired man dressed in tight-fitting gray cloth walked up to Samit and Capin Jeen. His quick, green eyes assessed them. Behind them stood a dark-haired woman, two younger men, and a small, blonde woman with large blue eyes.

"I am Captain Hans Daken of the Limon, commissioned by the Tregellion Alliance to make contact with worlds left bereft by the Great Chaos. To whom am I speaking, please?"

Samit opened his mouth to answer.

"I am Capin Jeen of the Starborn Clan. I am ruler of the raft city of Concordia on which you stand." She nodded toward Samit without taking her eyes off Captain Daken. "This is Maa Samit of the Waterborn Clan. He is head of the guard and chief law enforcer."

Captain Daken hesitated a moment. "In my culture it is customary to shake hands to show good intentions. I would like to shake your hand, Capin Jeen of the Starborn."

She carefully touched her hand to his, then clasped and shook it.

"Well met," Daken said with a smile that showed perfect teeth. "Maa Samit, I am pleased to meet you."

Samit grasped the soft, warm hand and shook it twice before letting go. He returned Daken's tight smile with one of his own.

"Is that a ship?" he asked the thin man.

Yes. We can navigate between planets, solar systems, galaxies, and even floating raft cities or islands. Please, allow me introduce my department heads."

The dark-haired woman, Numah, held the position of executive officer, a term the Concordians had heard only from the sacred texts. Rickan, the slight blond man with the ready smile, became the science officer. Dark-skinned, red-eyed Jaime was engineering officer. His sharp teeth reminded Samit of an evilfish.

The small, blonde woman asked Captain Daken a question in a different language before he had a chance to introduce her. He nodded assent with a quick smile. Samit suspected this woman was a favorite.

"I am Tama Lindbladden," she said in a clear voice. "I am the social scientist in charge of re-contact with lost peoples. We are very happy to find you." She smiled and stared at Samit.

He felt unclean and backward in front of these people, at a perfect loss for words. Her frank state and tight clothing caused his groin to twitch.

"Obviously your crafts and culture are well advanced compared to ours," Capin Jeen said smoothly, "but allow us to offer such hospitality as we can."

Samit's eyebrows went up for a moment and he glanced at his Capin in wonder and admiration. Her blood was beginning to tell.

"May our crew members mingle with your people?" Captain Daken asked. "They will be very respectful, I assure you."

"Of course!" Capin Jeen said instantly. "But I warn you, our people see strangers but once every eighteen-link."

"What's a link?" Tama asked instantly.

"A set is seven days," Samit answered. "A link is four sets, there are eighteen links in a full drift."

The woman thought for a moment. "That's a 504 day year, a bit over sixteen of our months. How do you measure smaller amounts of time?"

"Maa Samit," Captain Daken broke in, "perhaps you could

answer my officer's insatiable questions while we make our way to your place of authority?"

Samit glanced at Capin Jeen.

"Excellent idea," she said. "Let us depart for the Bridge Deck." She and the captain turned and walked toward the center of Concordia.

"Bridge deck?" Tama said. "I think I understand now! 'Capin' is form of 'captain,' and 'maa' must have evolved from em-ae-ae, which in old Federation ships stood for master-at-arms!" She became very excited.

Samit wondered if she realized she was treating on sacred wood, spouting off closed scripture like that.

"How long have you been on... what do you call this planet?"

Samit laughed despite himself. He turned to the stern-faced Numah walking on the other side of him. "Is she always this quick with questions?"

"Except when she's asleep," the woman said dryly.

"Wandered cultures fascinate me," Tama said softly. "I hope you don't think ill of me."

"Uh, no, I don't," Samit said. He glanced behind him. Many people rode down the tongue-ramp from the ship. His people were creeping out onto ten-ring, curiosity overcoming fear.

He turned back to Tama. "According to the Holy Log, our world is called Aquaria. We measure small time by spans, the length of time it takes the stars overhead to traverse the span of a man's hand."

"Fascinating!" she said gaily.

"May I ask you a question?"

"Of course."

"Is your ship safe from evilfish?"

"I'm not sure what you mean. What's an evilfish?"

"A large creature that lives in the water. They can swallow a man whole."

"How could they harm our ship?"

"Star metal drives them into a frenzy. They batter the craft apart with their bodies."

A small frown announced her doubt.

"And one of these things destroyed the ship that brought your ancestors here?"

"So the Holy Log tells us," he replied tersely.

"What was the name of your ancestor's ship?"

"*Jihad*."

"*Jihad*. Give me a moment. Library? History for seed ship named *Jihad*, old Federation registry, please." She spoke into the air beside her.

"Who are you talking to?" Samit asked.

"Comm link," she said brightly, holding up her soft gray collar to expose a small silver oval. "It's also recording everything I say or hear."

"Recording? It is capturing my words?"

"Why, yes. What's wrong with that?" Her large blue eyes were child-like. Suddenly her nose wrinkled. "Oh, what's that strange smell?"

"We're coming to the dirt rings. That's where night soil is collected and used to grow foodstuffs. We try to waste nothing on Concordia."

"In Limon, we have all of that done automatically, through tubes and pipes and stuff. We never have to see or smell it," she said apologetically.

"I would like to see your ship sometime."

"Oh, you will. Anyone who wishes can leave with us."

A cold heaviness settled in his chest. This would bring trouble. He didn't know how, but he knew it was coming.

Tama cocked her head to her comm unit side.

"Oh!" she said.

"What?"

"The *Jihad*, it was lost quite far out in uncharted space. Its final sub-space transmission said it was being attacked and needed assistance. Just a moment." She bent her head toward her collar again.

Samit noticed how soft her neck looked. Her words edged into his mind.

"So they did send a distress call," he said softly. "Why didn't anyone come to help?"

"The library says," she said, straightening up again, "that no attempt was made to find the *Jihad* before the Great Chaos began. It was too many parsecs away from any other ship."

"Parsec?"

"A measure of distance in space."

"You didn't answer my question about your ship."

"Oh, I don't think we have too much to worry about. These, ah, evilfish can be killed can't they?"

"Yes, but not easily."

"Your raft city seems to have lasted a long time."

"They don't attack ironwood, it's poison to them. We use ironwood spears to kill them."

"Well," she smiled warmly, "at this point we'll just assume our weaponry can subdue a few fish."

Samit pulled back into himself. The woman didn't believe him, didn't take his concern seriously. Being ignored ill-suited him.

Captain Daken spoke intently to Capin Jeen. Samit wasn't sure he liked that either, too much was happening too quickly.

Cassock Wye and his four chaplains stood outside East Chapel when the party approached. No protocol existed for something like this, no dogmatic cant to be followed to the letter. Samit wondered what the old gasbag would do.

Capin Jeen and Captain Daken slowed and then stopped in front of him, the rest of the party crowded around.

"Welcome in the name of the Ship!" Wye shouted, startling them all. He held up the Holy sigil with trembling hands. "Behold the Holy Image!"

"Why, that's a compass rose," Tama said softly. "Why is it holy?"

"Don't ask right now," Samit urged quietly. He felt unsettle, almost nervous.

"From where do you come?" Cassock Wye shouted. "And why?"

Jeen and the starship captain conferred quietly. Captain Daken stepped out, hand extended.

"I am Captain Hans Daken of the Tregellion Alliance. My ship is the Limon and we have come a great distance to welcome you back into the family of humankind. I would shake your hand in friendship."

The Cassock's heavy jowls quivered and his eyes rolled wildly. Samit thought he looked like a frightened goat tied for slaughter. "Are you of the Ship promised by scripture?" he shrilled.

Daken continued holding his hand out. "I don't know, I would have to see the scripture to answer that." His hand began to sag, then dropped to his side.

Cassock Wye stared at Capin Jeen for a moment, then at Samit. "I'm not sure it's meet that we show strangers holy writ."

"We'll wait on that for now," Capin Jeen said smoothly. "Would you like to accompany us to the Bridge Deck?"

"M-maybe later, my Capin." He disappeared into the chapel amidst a swirl of spice-scented, purple robes. The chaplains followed, glancing back in their retreat.

"Why is he so frightened?" Tama asked gently.

"All his life he has foretold the coming of the Ship, resurrection of the raft people, an accounting of sins and transgressions. Now you are here with a ship and you don't look much like gods, even to him. You have just gutted his world and he doesn't know whether to shit or swim for shore." Samit surprised himself with his words. He realized he could be speaking of himself as well as Wye.

"So you know there are landforms on this planet?" Tama said.

"Of course we do. Every eighteen links the drift takes us there. The raft cities began as extensions of the land. Food grew scarce and our ancestors were forced to cast loose to find more sea creatures after the drift proved to be reliable."

"When was that?"

"When my grandfather was a young man. The First Crew families are the rulers. The Landborn make star metal and trade it and ironwood for food from the sea. We know the sea well. It's a good life for most." Samit thought his words rang hollow.

"Fascinating!" Tama said breathlessly.

They arrived at the Bridge Deck surrounded by staring, quiet Concordians. Without further fanfare the party pushed through the crowd and into the official building.

"What happened then?" Rani asked.

Samit rubbed his scratchy eyes and yawned. "Mostly talk: agreements to exchange information, that sort of stuff. I need to get some sleep, Rani. Let me sleep for four spans and I'll answer all your questions, agreed?"

"But I heard things! I need to know if they're true," she said with an edge in her voice.

Water lapped soothingly under the house. His eyes closed of their own volition. "What do you need to know?" he asked drowsily.

"If we really can leave with them."

His eyes popped open. They burned with the effort of looking at her. Her jaw clamped down squarely, showing her stubbornness.

"What difference does it make?" he asked cautiously. "We live here."

"I'm not thinking about us, I'm thinking about Gordo." Rani hesitated for a moment and then words burst out like a spring shower. "He could be anything! He could travel to other worlds. He could be a starship captain instead of spending his life floating around on a smelly raft. This is *important*, Samit!"

Night cloaked the raft city. The day had been long, and he had had very little sleep. He silently cursed his exhaustion.

"I'm really too tired to talk about it now. They're not leaving in the next two days or anything. There's plenty of time to talk about it." He let his face fall into the pillow's oblivion.

A shriek woke him. He jerked to a sitting position and his hands shot out in the dim light, seeking his wife. Rani wasn't there, neither was Gordo.

Shouts spurred him into action. He pulled on his undershirt of softcloth and then the fishleather jerkin. For long moments his rough cloth trousers evaded him, but in less time than it seemed he cinched the ties and reached for his staff. After a second thought, he left the staff and darted outside.

Dawn leaked over East Chapel. The brightest stars were losing the fight for visual supremacy of the sky. Small Moon gleamed overhead. Large Moon had set.

A great mob of people lurched past his house, singing and yelling. Torches swung about with abandon.

Samit grabbed one of the revelers and spun him against the house. The man smacked into the wall with such force that his wind was lost and he sagged to a sitting position. Samit grabbed a handful of hair and pulled, forcing the man to look up. He recognized Tare, a leather worker from ten-ring.

"What is going on here?" he asked with a growl.

"Nuh-nuh-nothing!" tare gasped, trying to refill his lungs. "We're… just having a-a good time."

"You stink of spirits, where'd you get the drink?"

"The ship people have all we can hold. They say that the rules are finished, we can do as we please." A slight grin followed this outrageous statement.

"While you walk the streets of Concordia you follow the rules of Capin and Cassock!" Samit shouted into Tare's face. "And the Maa will make sure that you do!" He slammed the man's head against the wall again.

Tare slumped, unconscious. Samit stared after the carousing mob. His stomach rumbled sourly in anguished indecision.

Was Rani with them? No, she wouldn't take a small boy into a mess like that: but where were they?

He ran after the mob. Within a few moments he caught up with the stragglers. Slowing to a fast walk, he pushed through them, searching faces for first his wife, and secondly for anyone he knew well enough to question.

Many in the crowd were drunk on something with an odor he couldn't identify. Some were drunk on excitement. Hundreds of conversations jumbled in the air.

"I still don't think they're gods! Gods don't get drunk," said a drunken, pop-eyed man who reminded Samit of a spinefish.

"How do you know?" his companion countered. "If I were a god I'd be drunk all the time."

Samit hurried past them and found himself in the midst of a more serious argument. A tall thin man harangued two other men, and a woman.

"You would be stupid to stay here! These star-farers said they would train anyone in anything if they had enough aptitude. So why stay?"

"But, Kerf, what does that mean?" asked one of the men.

"Jema's right, said the other man. Maybe there isn't enough of this 'aptitude' to go around! I don't want to die a slave inside some ball of star metal."

"Aptitude means brains, intelligence. Everybody has aptitude in some measure," Kerf snarled.

"Yes, that's true," the woman said calmly. "But if my aptitude is for just bearing children or serving my husband, I think I would rather do it here where I can rely on the drift. The drift brings us all we want or need."

Samit grinned at her words and pushed ahead, searching faces. He noticed a stocky man who stood out in the crowd because he wasn't drunk or excited. He was observing all he could and stepped out of the way of the more active.

Samit peered at him and recognized Avik, the guardsman who found the sacrilegious only a day ago.

By the drift! So much has happened since then.

"Avik, what's happening?" Samit asked as he drew near the man." How did all of this start?"

"Maa Samit! Pardon me for not seeing you, but you don't have your staff..."

"I thought I could discover more without it."

"Yes, very wise. They have all lost their wits. Some of the star people asked for spirits. When they were told only the Cassock could dispense spirits, they laughed and went back to their ship.

"Soon they returned with many flasks and everybody began drinking. They don't know what is going to happen next. They are afraid and excited at the same time. What *is* going to happen next?"

Samit felt as if a strong north wind was blowing through his mind and soul, sending thoughts and emotions tumbling like so much dry seaweed. He stared at Avik's earnest face, who in turn stared at the maa in supplication. He suddenly hated the guardsman, wished he would go away and leave him alone instead of standing there asking impossible question.

"I, I don't know," Samit said finally, detesting the words. "There is much that the Capin, Cassock, and I have to talk about. And, of course, we have to talk with the strangers..."

"With all due respect," Avik waved his hand at the mass of people around them, "you'd best talk quickly, and soon."

First things first, he thought. "Have you seen my wife and son?"

"Yes. They went aboard the... the ship."

"What! Why?"

"I think you son was hurt–"

Samit ran, pushing through the crowd, cursing and striking at those who got in his way.

Gordo hurt. Rani and Gordo were aboard the ship. Would that huge, metal monster let them leave? Did Rani want to leave? Too fast, this was all happening too fast.

Two figures stood where the ramp touched the deck. Samit slowed and caught his breath, considered what should be done next. They looked as soft as their tight-fitting clothes, these star-men. Their hands lacked the horny callus left by honest toil and their dependence on magic seemed total.

He swallowed his apprehension and steadied his step as he approached the pair.

"Here comes another one," one of the men said.

"At least this one's not on his knees." They both laughed.

Samit had heard sentries laugh like that before.

"Good morrow," he said calmly, stopping in front of the men.

"In the name of the Lords of Tregella, we greet you," the taller of the two said formally.

"I believe my wife and son are aboard your ship."

"There are very few of your people aboard, sir," the shorter man said dubiously. "What are their names?"

"Rani, and Gordo. Of the Waterborn clan."

The tall man spoke into his collar communicator. Samit could tell when the answer came: both men suddenly had a distant gaze that focused on nothing.

"Ah, you must be the Maa. Samit, yes?" the short man was all smiles and welcoming.

"Yes, I am Samit."

"Your wife and son are aboard. Your son broke an arm an hour or two ago and the captain directed the ship's doctor to repair it. They're in sick bay, would you like to visit them?"

Samit stared up at the dark ship with its darker mouth licking his raft. He suppressed a shudder and nodded. "Yes. I want to see them."

"Just step on the ramp. Someone will meet you at the hatch and show you the way."

Samit nodded and stepped on the ramp as if he'd been doing it all his life. The ramp surface began to move smoothly, carrying him rapidly toward the circular maw of the ship. His heart lurched in his chest and he successfully fought the urge to jump over the edge and into the water.

His wife and son were in there. He had to get them out. As he neared the portal he suddenly wondered why he felt so negative about the ship. Rani thought it offered a better life.

I've spent most of my life looking past the surface, the obvious, to find the real reasons behind events, he thought. *It's hard to stop now.* He stepped off the top of the ramp and moved through a curtain of moving air.

Just from the smell, he knew he was inside the ship. The odor of metal permeated the interior. The light grew brighter by the second.

"Maa Samit of the Waterborn, welcome to the *Limon*."

He turned and looked into the face of Executive Officer Numah. Her long, dark hair was combed to a point that became a ridge, twisted around the top of her head and fluted back into her high collar. He wondered how it stayed in one place when she moved.

"Thank you, Numah. Pardon me, but I don't know your rank."

"Commander. If you'll follow me, I'll take you to your family." She turned without waiting for an answer and strode down the narrowing passageway.

Samit hurried to keep up with her while looking at as much of the ship as he could. A wealth of pipes covered the ceiling. Those that worked metal at Haven had lost the art of making pipe; troughs were the best they could do.

"Where was this ship built?" he asked her back.

"It was assembled at a shipyard in orbit around Jancey, which is in the Randolph System," she said over her shoulder.

He refused to ask where those places were; it didn't matter anyway. Her tone indicated that the she took the people of planet lightly.

"Where will your ship go next?"

"You'd have to ask the captain. I don't know."

They turned off the passageway and came to a doorway that led to nothing. There was no floor. Commander Numah stopped and turned to look at him.

"This is a drop shaft." Her fingers ran over a square of colored buttons. "I've set it for the medical deck. All we have to do is step in and it will *safely* lower us to where we want to go. Are you ready?"

"What will stop us?" he asked nervously.

"Something called an anti-inertia field. Trust me, it works." She stepped inside the space and fell from sight.

Putting his hand on the doorframe, he peered down. All he saw was blackness and nothingness. It was as if the ship had swallowed the commander.

He knew if he thought much more about it he would never follow her. He stepped in and tensed his body. Once he had stepped on a rotten ice floe in the Northern Sea and his body had sunk slowly into it. Other than being alarming and very cold, it had been an almost pleasurable sensation.

He suddenly experienced the same sensation, except this wasn't cold; it was warm. Abruptly his feet touched a metal deck again, he bent to look, lost his balance and fell. Numah's boots glistened with a mirror-like shine that Samit would have liked to examine further.

"Are you hurt?" she asked in her hard voice.

He scrambled to his feet. "No, I am fine. That was very... interesting."

"Some primitive peoples lose control of their bladders the first time. I'm glad you didn't."

"Maybe I'm not as primitive as others," he said shortly.

A small smile tugged at the edge of her mouth. "Perhaps not."

The walls no longer offered the metallic gray he had grown used to. They now reflected a gleaming white that didn't look metallic. He experimentally tapped a finger against it.

"They're ceramic with a Teflon glaze," Numah said. "They're easier to keep sterile than metal."

He peered at her. "Sterile?"

"Very clean." Her eyes swept over him before she turned away.

"Oh."

He followed her to a closed door. She put her hand on a shiny black plate on the wall and the door slid open silently. Numah stepped back and motioned him to enter ahead of her.

Samit obligingly went through the door. The small room was bare save for a bench along one wall. The door slid shut as he turned around. He was alone.

"Hey!" he shouted.

A woman's flat voice came from nowhere. "This is a sterilization chamber. Please disrobe and put your clothing in this chamber for cleaning." A piece of wall slid open. "While waiting for sterile clothing, please enter the bath and step out when instructed. Personnel will not be allowed on the medical deck until they have finished this procedure. Thank you."

Samit stared around angrily but found nothing other than the hole in the wall. He shrugged out of his tunic and threw it into the hole. His trousers followed a moment later. The wall slid shut and another panel slid open, revealing a chamber with glowing walls.

Feeling vulnerable, Samit stepped through the opening. The floor began to move, carrying him through a narrow hallway. Suddenly steaming water jetted at him from all directions, feeling like darts as it struck.

He closed his eyes and stolidly endured. The water ceased and a fine spray misted over him, then a warm, strong wind dried him. He had never felt this clean before in his life.

The wall in front of him snicked open and he entered a

different room. On a wall hook hung a suit of soft-cloth.

"Please wear the sterile suit provided," the hidden voice said. "Your cleaned clothing will be returned to you upon departure from the medical deck. Push the lighted panel when you are ready."

The short pants felt too snug at first, but rather than crush his genitals as he feared, the cloth seemed to contain and support them softly. The trousers and tunic were the softest garments he had ever worn.

The fastener eluded him for a few moments. He couldn't figure out how one side held the other, but finally he was satisfied that it wouldn't slip. The soft boots had the same sort of fastener to close the tops.

When he stood up again he felt so good that he grinned for a moment. Then he remembered where he was and regained his serious mindset. He pushed the small, glowing panel.

The door slid open to reveal Commander Numah talking to a small, dark, very pretty woman garbed in pale blue clothing just like Samit's.

"Maa Samit, this is Lieutenant Commander Sternad. She is the medical duty officer and will take you to your family." Numah turned on the balls of her feet and left the room.

Samit followed her with his eyes, and turned to the smiling woman at his side. "She doesn't like me, does she?"

"Commander Numah considers it her duty to dislike and distrust everyone with whom she comes into contact. She's like that with us, too. Please come with me, Maa Samit."

Her odor washed back over him as he followed her down a gleaming passageway. She smelled of warmth, mystery, and alien eroticism. Urges and desires buried for many drifts surged into his mind again.

Samit shook his head. He was here to see his family and, like some youth, he was thinking about going into rut! Still, it was difficult not to notice how Sternad's compact body moved under the blue softcloth.

She swung around and stared into his eyes. For a heart-stopping moment he thought she could read his mind. Her pupils were very large and she smiled.

"They're right in here, Maa Samit." She pressed her palm to one of the dark, shiny squares and the door opened noiselessly. He had trouble pulling his eyes from hers.

"Samit?" Rani said in wonder.

He wrenched his eyes from the alluring medical officer and looked into the room. Rani was standing by a bladder or tube in which Gordo lay unmoving. He hurried into the room and hugged her.

"What's wring with our son?" he asked into her hair.

"Oh, Samit. It's all my fault." She said brokenly.

His hands traveled up and he lifted her tear-stained face. "What's your fault?"

"There was so much happening. You were asleep and wouldn't wake up. So I sat by the door to watch all the people…" She was crying freely. "Gordo woke up from all the noise and asked me what was doing. So I said 'let's go see,' and we went."

"Went where?"

"To where the crowds were talking, singing, and drinking. They were all very excited. The ship people were telling stories about other worlds and how we could all go to those places and lead exciting lives."

"How did Gordo get hurt?"

"Someone shouted that it was all a trick. That all who went with the ship people would just be made slaves. A huge fight just– just was *there!* I grabbed Gordo and tried to run but the people around us began to hit and kick," her voice trailed off.

"Yes?" he prompted.

"This man, a big man, got hit in the side of the head and he fell on Gordo. I–I heard the bone in his arm break, and Gordo screamed. I pulled the man off Gordo. He wasn't even as heavy as he looked. The bone of Gordo's arm was sticking out through the skin and blood was everywhere." She shuddered and cried harder.

"How did you get *here?*"

"That woman from the ship, Tama. She was just suddenly there. She said, 'let me help,' and spoke into the air and soon there were others there who put Gordo on a thing that floated. His pain went away and he slept.

"They brought him here and put him in this chamber." She pointed. "It heals him quickly."

"How quickly?"

"By morning, they said."

"Do you still wish Gordo to go with them?"

"That's not what I said." Her tears stopped and she caught Samit's eyes with hers. "I said we must think about the opportunities he would have with the ship people."

"Last night, when the fight started, who yelled the thing about slaves?"

"I, I don't know. Everyone's voice was shrill and high, they were all excited and it was difficult to tell who said what."

"I need to find out," he said shortly. "When Gordo is well will you leave the ship?"

"If that is what you wish, my husband."

"I wish it." He pulled her to him and held her warm, familiar body. "There is something unspoken happening," he said softly in her ear. "Before we make decisions about Gordo's future, we must understand all of it."

"I agree," she whispered.

He stepped back. "I must see to my duties. I'll look for you both at home tonight."

"Yes, Samit."

He walked over to the door and put his hand on the black plate. The door slid open to reveal the short, dark shape of Sternad.

"Do you wish to leave now, Maa Samit?"

"Yes," he said, stepping through the doorway. She didn't back up as the distance between them closed. The door behind him slid shut.

She stared up at him, eyes wide and alive with interest. "Would you like a tour of the *Limon* on your way out?"

Samit was aware of her totality again. He was also aware that he was strongly erect and the softcloth didn't hide his condition.

"I–perhaps I should get back to my people." His mind swirled with lust and soft-focused fantasies.

She arched her back as she looked up at him. Her nipples showed plainly through the thin fabric over her breasts. He felt he would burst if he didn't so something quickly. For a moment he tried to focus on Rani, but overwhelming lust fogged his mind.

"Show me what you will," he said thickly, tired of fighting the demands of his body.

She reached out and ran a hand over the thin cloth that covered his engorged penis. "Follow me," she commanded softly.

Quickly they moved through corridors. At some point the walls changed back to gray metal, then to soft shades of blue and green. She stopped at a doorway and pressed her hand against the ubiquitous black panel. The door sighed open and they darted through.

The room measured less than half the size of his house. A large bed took up one corner. A desk with objects scattered in front of a glowing screen dominated the rest of the room. His attention focused on the woman.

Her tunic fell to the floor, revealing a supple body and large breasts for so small a woman, the nipples still fully erect. Beneath the smooth mound of her belly, dark, wiry pubic hair thrust out at him. She closed the distance between them.

"Let me help you." She pulled his clothing off easily, pushed her body against his, and rubbed her nose across his hairy chest. "My barbarian," she murmured.

Abruptly they were on the soft bed, smashing their bodies together in mutual frenzy, joined most amazingly. Once she pushed him away for a moment, gasped, "Wait, don't rush so!" Then she came to him again, more slowly, and their passion again spiraled back to the peak where this time they didn't stop.

Samit felt the molten rush through his loins and she pulled him to her as tightly as she could and screamed in abandon, "Oh, Janis!"

His ejaculation went on forever, the sensation of release pushing him to the edge of insanity before it ceased. He fell on her sweaty body, thoroughly spent. She laughed deep in her throat.

"Oh, you were as good as I knew you would be, my barbarian. Would you like to do that again?"

"I think that would probably kill me," he said. "I haven't been with another woman since I took a wife. But there seemed to be a force pulling me to you…"

She laughed again. "Do you dislike what we did? Are you angry?"

"I, I feel bewildered. I don't know why I came with you."

"I did it to you," she whispered. "Your body reacted to my pheromic essence. I can increase it when I wish."

"I don't understand."

"It's ancient, goes back to when our species lived like animals. One of the differences between male and female is smell, sexual smell. We all still have a little of it.

"I had mine altered so I can control it at will. When I saw you, I wanted you. So I increased it."

"You wanted me? Why?"

"You have a vitality that men on this ship don't possess. Your hands are rough, your attitude is no-nonsense, and you have physical strength from working with your body as well as your mind."

Samit felt a dull wonder that she had been inflamed this way about him. He also felt used – and violated. Anger stirred in his clearing brain.

"Why did you not ask me if I wanted to...?"

"It's more enjoyable this way," she said with a smoldering look. The tip of her tongue slid slowly across her lower lip.

Despite himself he felt desire building in the bottom of his belly again. She reached for him. He focused on his anger, rolled off the bed and quickly began to dress.

He stood facing away from her. "How do I get my own clothes back?" he asked over his shoulder. He pulled on the boots and fastened the tops.

"What do you want with that smelly fish skin? What you have on there will last twice as long and be three times as comfortable." Her voice drifted lazy and indolent.

He turned and looked at her. The slow rise and fall of the full breasts pulled at him. He moist pubis called for his manhood. "I would like to get my clothing. How do I do that?"

"Ask for it at the afterbrow."

"Afterbrow?"

"The place where you entered the ship. They'll have it for you."

"How do I get back there?"

"Ask the ship, it'll show you." She rolled over on her side and went to sleep.

Samit carefully flattened his hand on the black panel. The door slid into the wall. He stepped out and looked around. There was nobody in sight. The door closed behind him.

Feeling foolish, he spoke into the passageway. "How do I get to the afterbrow?"

"Follow the deck arrows." The curiously flat female voice said again, bland as day-old weedcake, and seemed to be in his head equidistant between his ears.

He looked down at his feet. A yellow arrow glowed beneath the surface of the deck. He took a step in the direction indicated and the arrow moved smoothly, one pace ahead of him.

This ship brimmed with magic. He followed the silent arrow through the maze of corridors, and passed crew members without comment, his mind awash with conflicting emotions. The doctor's blithe seduction told him much about these people.

If they would use his so casually, what would they do to those in meaner conditions on Concordia? Perhaps she was an aberration, or ill. Beneath his growing distrust of the ship people lay his disgust at his own actions.

More than ever he wanted Rani and Gordo off this perplexing craft. But could he explain why? How would he feel if Rani had been trapped by the smell of some handsome male?

"I wouldn't believe her," he muttered to himself.

"Wouldn't believe who, Maa Samit?"

He glanced up sharply to find Tama walking beside him.

"How long have you been with me?" he asked curtly.

"Just a brief span. I didn't mean to intrude. Would you rather walk alone?"

The hurt in her eyes and face were so guileless that he felt like a bully. "I apologize for speaking to you so harshly. I am angry at another and I struck at you."

"Why are you angry?" she asked instantly. "I mean, I'd like to help you if I could."

"You have asked me much about life on the raft. Now I want you to tell me about life on your ship, on your worlds, and what the people are like."

"Oh, my. That's a great deal of information. Perhaps you should have a session with the library."

"Is the library a ship's officer like you are?"

"No," she chuckled. It's a collection of information. A very large collection that can answer every question you or anyone else could ask about us and our worlds."

"How do I gather this information? Would it take me a long time?"

"If you accessed everything it would take you many drifts to read it. However you can ask questions about specific subjects, or read overviews of just one or two planets."

He frowned. This was getting far too complicated. His eyes caught hers and held them.

"Maybe you could just answer some questions for me?"

"Anything you want to know!"

"Is it your way to use someone's body without really asking?"

"What? How do you mean?" She glanced around them quickly, color high in her cheeks.

Sparingly, he told her of his encounter with Sternad. "Sometimes in Concordia a man ends up with a woman other than his wife, but at least both have agreed to the coupling. I, I feel wronged, even though I participated vigorously."

"I apologize, Maa Samit. Lieutenant Commander Sternad not only violated your person, but she has also committed a crime according to our laws. If you file an official complaint with the captain, she will be punished severely."

"What she did is not normal for your kind?"

"Not *my* kind, I assure you," she said with some heat. Her face softened again. "You see, there are people from many different worlds on this ship. People from the same world can be very different. The *Limon* has incredible diversity among its crew."

"So everyone on this ship is different? Some have tabus that others break?"

"I'm afraid so."

"Do you think I'm a barbarian or a primitive?"

"What? Barbarian! Primitive! Of course not. You are a product of a metal-and-technology-poor culture.

"What you and your people have done here is admirable and in harmony with your environment. Your beliefs are clearly traceable back to the ancient Judean-Christos ethic and the shipboard discipline of pre-chaos times."

He watched her as she spoke. Condescension and bright-eyed hunger didn't cloud her face as they had Sternad's. All he could see was honesty, admiration, and an urgency to explain. He decided he liked this small, quick woman.

"You don't think I'm a primitive barbarian then?"

She grinned suddenly. "No, absolutely not. However I think there are barbarians on this ship whom you should avoid."

He returned her grin, but his voice was somber. "What would they do with any of my people who decided to go with the ship?"

Her grin faltered, finally vanished. "That depends."

"On what?"

"Aptitude. Age. Basic intelligence. There are a lot of variables." Her eyes didn't seem as clear as they had a moment ago.

"If I decided to go, what could I look forward to?"

"There's the afterbrow. Let's go outside to finish this discussion." She hurried ahead of him.

"As you wish."

Two crewmen on duty nodded as Tama and Samit passed. He stopped and turned to the men.

"I would like my clothing."

One of the men pulled a package from a low shelf, handed it to him.

"There you are, Maa Samit."

He thanked the men and silently rode down the long ramp behind Tama. They stepped out of the shadow of the ship and the heat of the morning sun surprised his back.

A guardswoman in Capin's livery darted up. "Good morrow, Maa Samit." She saluted. "My pardon, but the Capin wishes to see you as soon as possible."

After his visit to the ship, Concordia seemed quaint and simple. With some difficulty he wrenched his mind back to the reality of his floating world.

"Lead. We will follow."

The guardswoman looked askance at Tama, but offered no reply. She executed a precise turn on the balls of her feet and marched off toward the Bridge.

"Would you accompany me, Tama? I would like to hear your answers to my questions."

"You may not like what you hear," she said flatly. "But I will answer them just the same."

They kept pace three meters behind the guardswoman. Samit listened while Tama spoke in a low, rapid voice. Her manner underwent a change–the bright, interested, wide-eyed innocent transformed to a world-weary, bitter woman.

"Where to start? If you were to go with the *Limon*, they would probably put you in the security section, as much to watch you as well as making use of your skills. If a returnee has high scores on the aptitude tests–"

"Wait. What is a returnee? What is aptitude? These words are new to me."

"A returnee is anyone brought into our culture. The rationale being that they were once part of our culture but were isolated by the Great Chaos."

He listened absently as she explained aptitude. The drunken man had been correct. Her answers generated new questions.

"What was this 'Great Chaos' you all speak of?"

"It was a war that spanned a century and five star systems. It began over a trade squabble between two subject worlds and expanded to their patron worlds. By the time the fighting stopped, three planets had been destroyed and technology declined to the point where it was considered heresy by a majority of the surviving cultures."

"How long ago did this happen?"

"Roughly three hundred years. It's taken the Tregellion Alliance a hundred years since redeveloping space flight to get this far, to find Aquaria, that is. However we think this was one of the last planets to be seeded before everything came apart."

Samit waited for her to continue as they followed the swiftly moving guardswoman. Her silence lengthened.

"What would they do with someone who had little aptitude?"

"If the ship took them at all, they would probably end up as heavy labor on one of the other frontier worlds," she said flatly.

"Then why come here at all with your stories of other worlds and your devices that do all your work for you?"

"Brains, Maa Samit, raw intelligence, and quick, trainable minds. Every planet has a percentage of genius, and that's why we're here."

Since the arrival of the ship a weight had been building on his shoulders. Now it doubled in mass, bending his spirit nearly to the breaking point. How could he prevent this thing from happening? The bright ones would go because they would realize how much more the Tregellion Alliance could give them than could Concordia, or even Haven.

"I told you that you wouldn't like my answers," Tama said quietly, her large eyes on his face.

Then they reached the Bridge Deck. The guardswoman turned and stopped them.

"Many pardons, Maa Samit," her eyes flicked to Tama then returned to his. "My orders are to bring you, alone, into the Capin's quarters." She looked back at Tama. "I ask your pardon, my lady."

Tama smiled quickly. "I'm glad that someone on this raft started using their brains." She turned and walked back the way they had come.

"Thank you, Tama," he called after her slumped shoulders. She didn't respond.

Samit hurried into the Capin's quarters.

"Maa Samit, thank goodness you've come back." Capin Jeen looked haggard. Her eyes hung bloodshot over purplish pouches, her hands shook like those of an old woman and he noticed ragged nails.

"Of course I came back. Did you think I would leave with those people?

"Your son is."

"No. He's only on that ship until his arm heals."

"Not Gordo," she said tiredly. "Ansul. He is organizing a band of young people to join the ship. They wish to leave Concordia forever."

"Ansul?" He saw his son as a boy again: bright, witty, completely self-assured and in control of those around him. Samit knew the boy would be a leader some day.

Perhaps if he had tried to bridge the gap between them this wouldn't be happening now. Ever since Semo's death Ansul had rebuked his father. One would almost think that Samit had been responsible for Semo's early death, rather than his brother.

Not good to think of this now, he decided

Perhaps he could talk to Ansul, explain how callous the ship people were to "returnees," and change his son's mind. He slowly became aware that Capin Jeen was speaking.

"...Tanu, Yuri, and even Darwayne are going with him. He even asked me if I would go." Her forlorn voice brought a lump to Samit's throat.

As children, Ansul and Jeen had been inseparable. Her father had been cool to the relationship. When Jeen became Capin upon his death, Ansul proposed marriage.

Jeen asked him for more time. She suddenly needed to learn quickly what once she had a lifetime to absorb. Stung and unreasoning, Ansul turned his back on her and took another to wife. Jeen had been devastated.

"What about his wife, is she going, too?"

"No. Ansul said he was leaving her here, with the rest of the dullards." Jeen's voice was apologetic.

"How many?"

"Almost a hundred. He was boastful. He–" She began to sob. Great wracking moans burst from her and she would have fallen if Samit hadn't caught her and held her fast to him.

"It's all muh, mu, my fault!" she wailed. "If I had married him–"

"He'd go anyway," Samit said with a growl. "He's not one to share, never has been. He would only hurt you like he's hurting, ah, his wife."

Samit never could remember the name of the tiny, dark woman who became his daughter-in-law. He preferred not to know the names of his son's victims. "Where are they now?" he asked finally.

"North Chapel."

"That figures," Samit said sourly. "That bird was probably his, too. Guess it's time that I went and had a talk with these people."

"Be careful, Maa Samit. Ansul said there was no way to stop them."

"Stop him, he means. There might be a few who will listen to reason and at least weigh my words before they leave."

"What will you say?" She dried her eyes and looked at him questioningly.

"I'm not sure yet," he said, not meeting her gaze and moving toward the door. "I'll think of something on the way."

"My pardon, Maa Samit, but I cannot let you enter." The young man set his face earnestly; the pike in his hands looked sharp.

Samit glanced over the guard's shoulder at the closed door of North Chapel.

"It's taboo to bear arms against the Maa, Tanu. You know that."

Tanu licked his lips and look around nervously. He looked over Samit's shoulder, not meeting his gaze.

"We, we're making our own rules now. We're leaving Concordia." He audibly swallowed. "Ansul said no one was to enter who had not agreed to leave with us."

"Maybe I'm leaving with you. Nobody's asked me yet."

"You'd leave with us? I don't think, I mean, you're part of what we wish to leave," Tanu blurted.

Before Samit could answer, the chapel door opened and Ansul eased out.

"Having some trouble, Tanu?"

Samit glanced at the guard's whitened knuckles, let his eyes travel the length of the pike, and finally looked into the face of his oldest child.

"The Maa says he wishes to come with us!"

Ansul's eyes didn't reflect the smirk on his lips as he stared at his father.

"No, he's only spreading night soil on you in hopes of growing something. Aren't you, father?"

"As I pointed out to your *guard*, nobody asked me if I wanted to go or not."

"Even if you would leave with us, I don't want you to go. You're too much of this," he jerked his head at the raft around them.

"You're right, I don't wish to leave. But I'd like to explain to you and your friends why I'll stay."

"We don't care to hear your words, Maa Samit. We know you're part of the established order. It's obvious why you wouldn't leave – they wouldn't let you be the captain's right-hand sealouse on the *Limon*."

Hate radiated from Ansul's core. There was no bridging this gap. His son was as lost to him as his dead brother.

"Oh, but they would. All I want is one span. I don't care if you choose not to listen, in fact I would prefer it. However the others in there bear me no animosity. Ask them if they would hear my words, or are you afraid they would follow me rather than you?"

The smirk snapped into a hard line. Ansul's jaw muscles bunched as he ground his teeth. Roughly he pushed Tanu aside.

"Let this old sea bird have his squawk. Then we can all bid him farewell as we leave this stinking wood pile for the stars."

Samit pushed past the two men and entered North Chapel. The drone of many conversations ebbed away as the crowded room became aware of his presence. Nearly two hundred people stood and stared at him as he stepped up on a bench.

"They want you because you're smart, you're trainable," he said without preamble. Many smiled and nudged their neighbor, a light buzz of comments filled the room.

"But have they told you what they want you to learn? In what tasks they will train you? Or what happens if you can't learn their lessons? Have you asked?"

The smiles disappeared, replaced by uneasy glances. Samit waited until the noise of shuffling feet stilled.

"I've been on the ship, the *Limon*. It is a wondrous thing, almost magic to my way of thinking. However there are those aboard her who have no regard for others. You would be merely a tool or a toy as far as they're concerned." He stared from one person to another, touching as many as possible with his gaze.

"If you don't meet their needs mentally, they will use you physically. You could easily end up as heavy labor on some other world. You could become a slave no matter what your 'aptitude' is."

"But if we have the aptitude for a skill, would we become a citizen of the ship?" asked someone in the back of the crowd.

"I don't know. Just keep in mind that some slaves don't do heavy work."

"Wait!" Ansul shouted. "Your questions will be answered before you go on the ship. There is someone coming–"

The door behind Samit swung open.

"Here he is now," Ansul said happily.

Samit turned and found himself looking down at Captain Daken. Jaime and Tama flanked their captain.

"Maa Samit, I didn't expect to find you here," Daken said.

"Nor did I expect to find you trying to steal my people, captain." He stepped down to face the man.

"Steal!" he said with a laugh. "I was invited here to talk to those who are interested in journeying to the stars with us. No one will come with us who does not wish to, I assure you of that."

"When does a person get tested for their aptitude?" Samit asked mildly. "Before or after the *Limon* leaves Aquaria?"

"Oh, it would be after. It isn't just one test, it's a series of tests that cover the entire spectrum of human knowledge."

"What happens to those who fail?"

"Nobody *fails* everything. It's impossible."

"What happens to those who score high?"

"Well," Daken grinned and clasped his hands in front of him. "There are so many opportunities for people in the technical science fields that I could spend a whole day listing them and then I'd probably leave something out."

"What happens to those who have poor aptitude in the technical science fields?"

"There's social science, hydroponics, food services, logistics, law enforcement; why the list just goes on and on."

"You left out heavy laborer, mining, and those other fields where brawn is more important than brains. What sort of a future does that hold for my people?"

Daken's eyes narrowed and grew cold. "I don't know where you get your information, but we don't need people for those fields."

"You may not need them. However don't you *exchange* crew members to other worlds in return for whatever you do need? Crew members that are of no real use to you?"

Tama gazed at his face, a smile tugged at the edge of her mouth.

"Sometimes people elect to leave the ship and settle on one of the hundreds of inhabited planets in the Alliance," Captain Daken said carefully.

"Can your crew members leave any time they wish and settle on any planet they wish?"

"Within reason. If we go to great lengths to train someone, we expect to receive the benefit of their skills for a certain period of time."

"On Concordia, we call that an enlistment. Ours last for the length of one drift. How long do yours last?"

"That depends on the skills imparted. Some enlistments last one ship's year, some last six."

"Is there a place on your ship for those who tire of their labors and sleep all day?"

"Of course not. What an absurd question! Everyone earns their keep on the *Limon*."

"What happens if they are injured or impaired and can no longer perform their tasks?"

"Depending on their length of service they are pensioned off on a planet."

"What planet?" someone in the back of the group asked. "Could we come back to Aquaria if we wished?"

"Of course, if there was a ship coming this far out. You must realize that this is the first visit by any ship in three hundred years. It may be years before we or any other ship visits here again."

"So this may be our only chance in our lifetimes to go to the stars, right?" Ansul asked quickly.

"That could easily be the case. We will be here for just three more days before we start back to the home worlds of the Alliance. You must decide by then."

Daken turned and left the chapel. Jaime followed immediately. Tama stood for a moment, staring at Samit, before she also left.

Everyone in the room tried to speak at once. Samit glanced at Ansul who returned a fierce grin.

"It looks like you lose, old man!"

"That remains to be seen," Samit said wearily. He pushed through the door into cleansing sunlight. Time to go get his wife and son.

"Maa Samit!"

He squinted into the afternoon sun for the source of the call. In the heavy shadows between two houses a hand motioned for him to approach.

"Come speak with me in the street," Samit called.

"There are too many eyes out there. By the Holy Sign, approach."

He glanced around. The street was empty even of children. Where was everybody? He moved slowly toward the shadows.

"Who wishes to speak to the Maa?" he called.

"Cassock Wye," the voice whispered loudly.

Even when he was a youngster Samit thought the official religion lacked feeling. The more years he gained, the more convinced he became that this faith served only those operating the Bridge Deck and Chapels. As the Maa, Samit kept his feeling to himself for the good of Concordia.

Wye hated him because the Maa wouldn't pay open obeisance to the church. Jeen's father had shared Samit's attitude, but never in public. Change died along with the late capin.

"I have come half way. You come out here to talk to me."

A pike point glinted in the shadows, reminding him that he stood unarmed. Cassock Wye trudged out from between the two houses, stopping at the hot edge of the shadow.

"There is heresy afoot!" Wye said in his excited, high-pitched voice. Behind him two men-at-arms stood in the shadows. "These starfarers are false prophets who are breaking the tabus of Concordia."

"Which tabus are those? The ones you have about exposing the truth in a factual manner? You're just scared that nobody will ever take you seriously again. If I were you, I'd be scared, too."

"Concordia needs the church! These people need the direction of steady minds and clear thinkers."

"There seems to be a new church growing from the people." Samit spat on the wood between them. "The only clear thoughts you ever had were about how to gain more power in this city. It's certain that we're going to lose some of our people to the ship, but maybe that will be a good thing. Most of those leaving are malcontents anyway."

"It is tabu to leave Concordia without dispensation from the *true* church! The Holy Log states–"

"The Holy Log is a copy of events and rules that have become completely outdated. Concordia, the other raft cities, even Haven are not the sum of creation any more – now we're just a small part of it. The sooner you accept that the better off you'll be."

"What we need is a provocation, an event that will take the people's minds off the marvels and free spirits provided by the ship's crew. Something that will enrage them enough to smite the false prophets," Wye shrilled.

"What in the drift are you talking about?"

The two men eased out and flanked Wye. Each held a pike at the ready.

"The disappearance of the Maa is what I'm talking about. The last time anyone saw him he was on his way to retrieve his wife and child from the ship of false prophets."

"You wouldn't dare try that! If you fail, you're a dead man."

"I think," Wye said smoothly, "…that you're the dead man."

Samit knew that the next words from Wye's mouth would order his death. There were two of them, both younger than him – he couldn't outrun them. That left one thing to do.

He attacked them.

"Kill hi–" Wye screeched as Samit's shoulder caught the heavy man in the chest. The Cassock lurched to the side and collided with the man on his left. Both hit the deck in a jumble of robes, limbs, and the unbending end of an ironwood pike.

The second man-at-arms quickly parried and slashed at Samit's head with the butt of his pike. Samit hesitated and then ducked under the arc of wood. He reached out, grabbed the left arm, pulled the man off balance and brought his knee up into the groin with as much force as he could.

The pike fell from nerveless hands and the man emitted a high shriek before crumpling to the deck. Wye scuttled into the shadows on all fours. The other man sprang to his feet and charged Samit, pike point first.

Samit feinted to his right. The man changed direction to meet the threat. The Maa threw himself to the left, landing on the unattached weapon and grabbing it as he rolled over and onto his feet again.

The first man lay on the deck in a fetal position, face white and open mouth struggling to catch his wind. He made an excellent obstacle for the second man to negotiate while trying to attack.

Samit backed rapidly into the street and took a defensive stance facing the sun. The pikeman only hesitated for a moment then charged. The weapon Samit held was tipped with star metal. Steel, Tama called it.

The steel was smooth, sharp, and polished to scintillating brilliance. Samit had already found the focal point of its reflection before the man began his screaming charge. He waited until the man took his third step before blinding him with reflected light.

He stepped to the side, easily evading the other's weapon, ran his point into the man's chest, and jerked it free. With a gurgle the man stumbled, fell, and died. Blood gushed from beneath the body.

The first assassin slowly pulled himself to his feet, a dagger in his hand. Samit smashed him in the side of the head with the butt of his pike, blood sprayed over the Maa, and the man fell face down, hands and legs twitching.

He plunged into the shadows, seeking Wye. The copper scent of blood filled his nose. His pulse pounded in his ears and his senses tingled, sharply alive.

The heavy odor of drying weed and the faint stench of night soil hung in the thick, hot air between the houses. Water lapped gently in the unseen channel between three-ring and four-ring. The smooth grain of the deck slid under his feet caressingly, pulling him forward.

The houses of Concordia were built close together, but it was tabu for them to touch. The law said a man must be able to walk completely around his house so that fire could not easily spread.

The resulting warren of small alleys splitting off from each other in the shadows could hold an army. Wye could be anywhere. However in order to escape he had to cross one of the catwalks between the rings.

Samit knew the Cassock would try for the nearest catwalk between three-ring and four-ring. Cautiously he edged in the direction of the crossing, pike at the ready. His eyes flicked back and forth seeking movement.

Wye was right; the disappearance of an authority figure could incense the Concordia. He grinned as he calculated how few would be upset by the absence of Cassock Wye. A faint sound brought his to a stop at the corner of a house. He listened, holding his mouth open wide so the blood pounding in his ears would be softer.

A garment rustled seductively around the corner. Samit glanced around quickly. Concordia seemed empty; there was nobody to be seen. A small wave slapped the edge of the ring, now visible a house-length away.

With a great bound Samit jumped out and away from the corner. A flash of light and the swish of a great-axe whispered past his ear. The axe head bit deep into the deck.

Cassock Wye hunched over, hands tugging futilely on the long axe handle, his mouth hung open, eyes round and staring at Samit from his ashen face. "No," he croaked, "it is tabu to touch the Cassock."

Samit smiled and fiercely drove his pike deep into the man's body.

"Everybody breaks a tabu now and then," he grated through clenched teeth.

Cassock Wye fell silently on the deck and blood poured from his mouth. His feet drummed rapidly for a moment, throwing off one of his sandals. Then he shuddered and died.

Samit grabbed the bare foot and dragged the corpse down the alley to the water between the rings. He saw movement on the other ring and quickly squatted out of sight. After a few breaths he poked his head up, no movement.

Quickly he pulled the body over to the edge and eased it into the calm water. In a swirl of purple robes it sank, leaving a faint line of blood that dissipated quickly. Samit dropped the pike and watched it arrow after its victim. The great-axe followed.

Suddenly he was so weak that his legs wouldn't support him. He dropped heavily on the deck and with shaking hands pushed out of sight of the other ring. His heartbeat slowed considerably and exhaustion pulled at him.

The urge to sleep was nearly overpowering, like Sternad's sex smell. Shaking his head angrily, he grunted to his feet and stumbled back to dispose of the two dead men-at-arms.

"Cassock Wye is missing, Maa Samit."

"Missing? What do you mean?" He didn't stop staring at the *Limon*. For the three spans since his encounter with Wye, he had stood in the East Chapel guard tower watching the dull, black ramp that led to the ship.

"The heliograph from the Bridge says that Cassock Wye cannot be found anywhere on Concordia," the sergeant of guards said.

"Did they ask you to look for him here at North Chapel?"

"Men-at-arms in the Cassocks livery came through here about a span and a half ago. They didn't say what they wanted, but then they never do."

"And you think they were looking for him, huh? What did they expect us to do about it?"

"I guess that's up to you, sir." Puzzlement shaded the sergeant's tone. "Do you have any orders for us?"

"Just keep watching that ship. No more of our people are to go aboard without speaking to me first. Put two armed guards at the bottom of the ramp."

"As you wish, sir." Puzzlement had given way to surprise. "What about the crew of the ship, do we allow them off?"

Samit thought hard for a moment. "Yes, but I want them followed. Send a message to the Bridge that I want three more ten-ranks of guards sent over here immediately."

"Yes, Maa Samit."

"Sergeant, tell them to wear battle-dress and bring pikes and cross-bows."

The sergeant acknowledged his orders and sped away to the signalman.

Now it begins, Samit thought. *It has to end soon.*

The ramp surface began to move.

Not until he saw Rani and Gordo riding down to the deck did he realize he was holding his breath. He slid down the pole and hurried out of the tower compound. Wife and son saw him as they stepped off the ramp.

In a heartbeat they were both in his arms.

"Daddy, Daddy! They fixed my arm! Look!"

"Oh, Samit, I am so glad to be with you again," Rani murmured into his neck.

He held them close, knowing he was doing the right thing, knowing that he must protect not only his family, but all of his people. When his eyes traveled upward, the *Limon* dominated the East Chapel waterfront like a madman's dream.

"Come, we must not stay here."

Rani moved with him, but she voiced her confusion. "Why? Is there a problem that I don't know about?"

"Much has happened." As he ushered them along the road to home, he told Rani about the meeting with Ansul and his followers, about Captain Daken skirting the truth, and that Cassock Wye had disappeared.

"Well, *that* shouldn't bother you!" she said with a snort. "You've never liked that man."

"The point is," he said carefully, "is that the Cassock is part of Concordia, an important part to some people's way of thinking. And everyone knows he wouldn't go on that ship unless his life depended on it." How easily the fantasy slipped from his lips!

"Do you think they kidnapped him? Why would they do that?"

"Wye was preaching against the ship. He said it was full of false prophets. Maybe some of them took umbrage."

"They wouldn't do that! They are here to help us, Samit. Why does everyone distrust them so?"

"Rani, they only want our best and brightest. If they don't master the skills the ship needs, they'll be put to work on some other planet as heavy laborers, dung spreaders, or who knows what. This is a raid. We have to accept that."

"Samit, I've always listened to you and I've always honored you. However you're looking at this thing sideways. There will be other ships visiting now that we're found again. Our people who go to the stars will be able to return for visits…"

"I'm not letting those people take *two* of my sons away," he said.

"Two? Oh, Ansul has decided to go, hasn't he?"

Samit nodded. "They can have Ansul, he's as good as dead to me anyway. Gordo stays."

"This might be his only chance to be something more than we are! How can we arbitrarily decide against it without talking about it?"

"If and when other ships visit Concordia, we'll consider sending our son to the stars. In the meantime the college at Haven can teach him about his own world. He has many drifts before he'll be ready to go anywhere. Why are you pushing him away?"

"I'm not! I just want what's best for him. Is that wrong?"

Samit looked down at his quiet son. "Gordo, do you want to go away with the ship, or stay here with us?"

His blue eyes filled with tears and he looked up at Rani. "Mamma, do I have to go away from you and Daddy?"

Samit knew he had won, even though unfairly. Rani dropped to her knees and hugged Gordo.

"Of course not! We were just talking about what would be best for your future. We wouldn't send you away if you didn't want to go."

"I don't want to go, Mamma," he said with a sniff.

"C'mon, let's got home," Samit said around the lump in his throat.

They moved on, each happy to be with the other two. In the distance Samit noticed people emerging from East Chapel, a lot of people.

"Now what?" he said absently.

"What are all those people doing in church?" Rani asked.

"I don't know; it's not even Bellday."

The stream of people moved toward them, obviously on their way toward the guard tower and the *Limon*.

"Rani, I want you and Gordo to avoid these people and go home by way of South Chapel, okay?"

She was about to question, he could feel it building in her. Then she read his face first. "As you wish, Samit. Please be careful."

Jael moved close to setting in the west. Long shadows stretched toward East Chapel guard tower. Samit stood in the middle of the street, watching the crowd move toward him, and he wished he had kept one of the pikes or had brought his staff with him.

When the crowd was ten paces away he held up his hand and shouted, "My people! Where are you bound?"

A man wearing guardsman livery stepped forward. "Maa Samit, we are going to banish the star people from Concordia."

Samit blinked slowly. "What?"

"They must leave. We don't want them here any longer. They've brought strife and discord. They don't care about our way of life, or the seasons, or the beauty and meaning of the Way of the Drift…"

"That's the name of the new religion, isn't it?"

"Yes, Maa Samit. We feel at peace with the Way. Let the hypocrites and wind-catcher fanatics leave on their magic ship. We've never needed it or them."

"Well said, Warli," Samit said, glad he remembered the man's name. "…but how would you expel these people from Concordia? Force of arms won't work; they have mighty weapons."

"We'll just tell them to leave, Maa Samit."

"I think I should go with you."

"Do you agree with our purpose, Maa Samit?"

He grinned at them. "I thought I was the only one who felt that way."

Relieved laughter came from many.

"Lead us, Maa Samit," a voice called.

He turned toward the *Limon* and swept his arm forward.

As they marched toward the East Chapel portion of ten-ring, Samit roughly counted the crowd. He concluded there were over five hundred. Pride swelled in his chest.

He entertained no doubts that the ship could kill them all. If he had to die over this thing, this was the way to go – at the front of his people. The ship loomed large on the darkening horizon and the hull gleamed black in the last rays of Jael.

Lights glowed inside the *Limon* and Samit could see figures moving quickly at the afterbrow.

They're getting ready for us. This is going to be a slaughter of innocents.

He fiercely wished a way existed that he could become the sacrifice for his people, and expel the "visitors" from their planet. No, on second thought, sacrifice was what the Cassock had come up with and it hadn't worked. New times called for new methods.

They poured over the catwalk onto ten-ring and began to fan out across the waterfront and between the buildings. Guardsmen emerged from East Chapel tower and mingled with the civilians. A sergeant spotted Samit and ran over to him.

"Maa Samit, more people are on their way from West Chapel and South Chapel. In the last span a number of ship people have gone aboard that we didn't even know were in the city. None have come off since then."

"Well done, sergeant. Place your men and women in the front rank. Help relay orders and direct the civilians."

"Yes, sir!" He instantly vanished in the milling crowd.

Samit raced up to the gangplank and turned to face his people. Large Moon budded slowly over the horizon, reflecting light across the darkening waterfront. Torches appeared in the crowd, giving the scene an almost festive air.

He raised his hands over his head, palms outward. The crowd quieted down from front to back. In a few heartbeats the only sounds were those of the sea and snap and crackle of the torches burning heavy fish oil.

"My friends, neighbors, relatives. We are here for a single, united purpose. We want this ship to leave us now, and leave our people here."

In the distance he could see another throng, torches bobbing in the night, moving purposefully toward them, West Chapel or South Chapel, coming to help. He felt drunk on emotion.

Samit turned and looked up at the afterbrow. There were no lights in the portal, but he knew armed crew lurked there.

"I want to speak to Captain Daken," he shouted. "I want to avoid bloodshed."

"He's on the way!" a panic-laced voice shouted out of the dark. "Just make them stop. We'll do anything!"

"What's he talking about?" Samit murmured to himself.

A great light flashed under the water and a towering gout of steam erupted from the surface of the sea, showering the waterfront with hot water. The hundreds of people on ten-ring began shouting and talking as they moved back away from the raft edge.

Another flash of light turned the depths into a parody of day. As the second gout of steam blasted from the roiling surface, Captain Daken hurried down the gangplank.

"Maa Samit! He thundered. "We'll do whatever you wish – just stop them!"

"My people have done nothing. I don't know where the great lights are coming from."

"The light is from our laser weapons. We're trying to drive off those creatures."

"Creatures?"

"Great huge things with a mouth big enough to stand in, full of teeth that look like daggers!" he shouted. "They're attacking my ship and they're damaging it!"

"Evilfish! I told Tama that they destroyed the *Jihad*, but she didn't believe me."

"Is there any way to kill them or drive them off?"

"What about your weapons? Aren't they working against them?"

"The water absorbs the strength of our fire. All we're doing is making steam! How is it that your raft hasn't been attacked?"

"They avoid ironwood. It's poisonous to them. But legend says they will attack anything else."

The *Limon* moved slightly, causing the gangplank to quiver. Another flash lit up the water. This time Samit happened to be looking down and saw the great hull curving away into the depths – as well as the silhouetted forms of two evilfish.

"If we help fight them, you must leave immediately, and without any of our people," Samit said swiftly.

"Agreed, how do you kill them?"

"I need to talk to my people. How do you make your voice loud?"

"Up here, quick."

Samit ran up the metal ramp. When he reached the top, Daken was holding out a small square of metal.

"Just speak into it."

"People of Concordia!" he said loudly. His voice thundered across the throng, hushing it. Faces turned upward toward him.

"The ship will leave if we help drive off the evilfish. Get your gear and launch your boats. There are at least two of them down there, maybe more. Hurry!"

The crowd fragmented purposefully as men ran into darkness where boats rested.

"How do you kill them?" Daken asked again.

"With large crossbows mounted in wood boats. It takes four men to row each boat, and two to shoot the weapon. However we have never hunted them at night. Can you provide light?"

"We were afraid to turn on underwater lights for fear of attracting more of the monsters."

"But you can provide light when we need it?" Samit pressed.

"Yes, anything you want."

"I want this visit wiped from your log. We wish to continue the drift and not worry about the stars. Come back in a hundred years and ask my grandchildren if they want the stars, but leave us alone."

"As you wish, Maa Samit. By the way, Lieutenant Commander Sternad has been reduced to lieutenant, junior grade, and fined half a year's pay for what she did to you."

Samit shrugged. The guilty memory of her wildly bucking body flashed through his mind before he concentrated on the launching of the boats.

Three boats already moved out to the edge of the *Limon*. Two more slid down the launch ramps and splashed into the dark sea as Samit watched. The first three went out of sight around the far edge of the ship.

"Is there any place I can stand so I can see all of my boats?" Samit asked quickly.

"Yes, follow me!"

Once again Samit plunged into the bowels of the *Limon*, hard on the heels of Captain Daken. In a very short time they came to the drop tube. Daken's fingers ran over the colored numbers.

"You've used this before, right?"

"Yes," Samit said tersely.

"Good!" Daken vanished.

Samit waited a moment then stepped into the void also. Pretending he was sliding down a tower pole, he kept his back straight. This time he didn't stumble when he reached the bottom.

"This way." Daken was running again. Samit followed, mentally revising his opinion of the star farers. He felt winded while Daken ran effortlessly, as if stamina flowed as common as seawater.

"In here."

Great windows looked out upon the dark depths. Something darker flowed past the transparent wall and hit the ship. Thunder boomed immediate and terrifying.

Somewhere a hissing started.

"The skin's punctured!" a voice shouted. "Seal the compartment."

"That makes three compartments breached," Daken said in a low voice. "If we turn on our lights you will be able to see the bottom of the boats, and the creatures."

"Make it happen!"

"Hull spots – full illumination," the captain said into his collar button.

The dark water lit with awesome brilliance. Samit had never witnessed a waking nightmare before. Evilfish swarmed everywhere.

The lights drove them into a frenzy and they hurled their long, armored bodies against the *Limon*, two and three at a time. An ironwood shaft knifed through the water and caught an evilfish in its middle eye. It jinked off into the stygian depths, trailing viscous liquid.

Then two of the creatures were hit at the same time and they battered through the middle of the swarm, injuring at least three more. One with a gaping maw easily four paces across rushed toward the window where the humans stood transfixed.

"Look out – it could come through!" a crewman screamed.

Samit stumbled backward, tripped on an immovable object and fell. He saw the evilfish smash through the great window just before his arm struck another immovable object and broke with a dull crack.

Samit nearly fainted in agony. The evilfish slid into the ship, snapping and writhing. Water roared through the great smashed window.

"Kill that damn thing!" Daken screamed. "Then get out of here!"

A burst of sharp retorts pierced the water's bellow and the evilfish stiffened and went limp. Water rushed around Samit and buoyed him. He didn't know where to go.

Daken half swam, half ran over to him.

"Follow me, Maa Samit. We've got to get out of here." He turned and began climbing a metal ladder attached to the wall.

Samit made it up two rungs before the weight on his broken left arm jerked a cry from him and he fell back into the swiftly rising water. With an effort he grabbed the ladder with this right hand.

"Samit?" Daken said, looking down. "What's wrong?"

"My arm is broken." His voice sounded strained and weak to him. "I fell when the evilfish…"

Daken dropped off the ladder and splashed next to Samit, going completely under before bobbing back up. Samit noticed that the water was level was nearly to the ceiling. The ladder ended at an open hatch, above which men waited with frightened eyes.

"We have to close the hatch! Hurry!"

"Get on the ladder," Daken gasped. "I'll push from behind."

Holding his left arm close to his side, Samit pushed himself up and, as soon as he felt Daken's shoulder dig into his butt, he grabbed the next rung to repeat the process. The remaining five rungs took all the energy he had left. Quick hands reached down and hauled him up.

Someone grabbed his broken arm and this time he did faint.

"Maa Samit, I hate to waken you, but we must talk."

Samit's eyes obediently opened and he peered into the face of Captain Daken. He glanced past the captain and realized he was once again on the medical deck. His arm felt warm but not painful.

"Usually we let a patient sleep off the regeneration process, but…"

"…we must talk," Samit finished.

"Let me help you up. We can go to my office."

In moments they walked down the gleaming white corridor. Whatever they had given Samit to wake him up had already cleared his head.

"I promised you that I would leave and not take any of your people with me, but that is proving difficult."

"Why is that, captain?"

"There are some who insist they have the right to leave with us."

"My son, Ansul, is one of them, isn't he?"

"Ansul is your son?"

"Only in flesh. How many others?"

"Five."

"Do you wish to take them?"

"They seem an intelligent lot. I think they might do well with us."

"Good. Take them with you."

"Thank you. Would you like something to eat or drink? My cabin is close."

"What happened to the evilfish?"

"The one that nearly got us was one of the last to die. They must have some intelligence because the rest fled. Our biologists and science people dissected it and think they can show you an easier way to kill the brutes."

"How long was I unconscious?"

"About five hours – sorry, I don't know how many spans that would be."

"It doesn't matter. You mentioned a drink?"

In the captain's comfortable quarters they drank a toast to life. Samit was about to propose a second toast when a chime sounded.

"What–" Samit said.

"Someone wishes to enter," Daken said softly. He raised his voice, "Come."

The door slid silently open to reveal Tama.

"The duty officer said you were here, she said nervously. "I, I have something to ask of you both."

"Would you like a drink, Tama?" Captain Daken asked.

"No, thank you, captain. Hans."

Samit caught the look that swiftly passed between them.

"You wish to stay on Concordia, don't you?" Captain Daken said.

"If it's all right with you and Maa Samit," she said in a small voice.

"I have nothing to say about it," Samit said quickly. "You have to ask Capin Jeen."

"She has given me her permission – but only if you agree."

Samit looked at the ship captain.

"Would you like to speak to Tama alone?"

"Yes," he said not taking his eyes off the woman, "but give her your answer first.

"I don't know why you would want to give up all this," Samit gestured, "for life on Concordia..."

"Oh, that's easy," she said fervently. "I am a social scientist. Here is an established culture that has just gone through a force-fed age of enlightenment. Most cultures go from that into a flowering, a renaissance. I think yours will, too, and I very much want to be a part of it. I want to record it."

"I would like that Tama Lindbladden. Welcome to Concordia." He stood and shook Captain Daken's hand. "Thank you, sir. I am honored to have known you. Safe journey."

Just as the door slid shut behind him, Samit heard Daken say, "Tama, how can you leave me?"

"The repairs are finished," Tama said, looking up from her comm link, "and they've finished downloading a copy of the library."

"Where will we get the power to run the library machines?" Capin Jeen asked.

"Solar collectors," Tama said with a smile. "They'll also light your homes some day, as well as cook your food."

"Maybe some day we'll build our own starship," Rani said lightly.

Samit frowned at her.

"Out of ironwood?"

"The ship is getting ready to take off," someone shouted from the door.

Capin Jeen, Tama, and Samit all rose as one from the table and moved out into the light.

"Daddy, look!" Gordo pointed at the *Limon*, floating about

two thousand meters from Concordia. It still looked big.

"Darwayne, Tanu, Yuri, his wife Sharz, their son Brun, and Ansul," Rani said in his ear. "I think we have profited from this encounter."

"I agree. I hope he's free of his hate."

Limon shot into the sky with a great thunder and boiling of water. The ship accelerated up, impossibly going faster and faster. Quickly it dwindled, leaving only a trail of vapor that dissipated in the wind.

Light flashed from East Chapel tower.

"The red fish are running!"

The crowd scattered in all directions, leaving Samit with the three women and his son. He looked at Tama.

"When does the flowering begin?"

"It already has. I've begun writing the true chronicle of Concordia and her people. I may even stay at Haven for one drift to do research. But I would like to operate the library and have Concordia be my home from now on."

"I hope you will be as happy here as my son will be on *Limon*."

A piercing, thin scream cut across their ears. All looked up to see the spacecraft high up at the edge of the sky, burning like a coal before disappearing out of the atmosphere.

"It *is* lyrical," Samit said absently, putting an arm around Rani.

Photo by Del Buhrman, DragAndFly Photography, LLC

Stoney and Colette Compton, along with their cats and two dogs, live in Oregon's Willamette Valley after nearly six years of living in much warmer and drier places. They are happy to be back in the Pacific Northwest.

Stoney participates in many science fiction & fantasy cons in Oregon and Washington, do feel free to tell him your opinion of his work. Colette teaches advanced ballet and competition performance to a select few.

Colette is also Stoney's first reader and initial editor which he greatly appreciates.